Pride Publishing books by Trina Lane

Single Books
Taking the Chance
Love's Return

Perfect Love
His Perfect Partner
Capturing Perfection
Simply Perfection
The Perfect Balance
The Taste of Devotion
The Sound of Salvation
An Imperfect Reunion

The Heart of Texas
Shards in the Sun

Collections
Totally Five Star: Turkish Delights

I0542492

The Heart of Texas

WINDOWS IN THE MIST

TRINA LANE

Windows in the Mist
ISBN # 978-1-78651-846-0
©Copyright Trina Lane 2019
Cover Art by Cherith Vaughan ©Copyright July 2019
Interior text design by Claire Siemaszkiewicz
Pride Publishing

Published in 2019 by Pride Publishing, United Kingdom.

WINDOWS IN THE MIST

Dedication

For anyone who was ever told they didn't
deserve a happy ending because of some mistakes
they made along the way.

Prologue

October 2016

The moment Javier opened the door to the Citadel, the restless energy that had been eating at him from the absolute shit day he'd had at work calmed. This was a place he understood. The rules were simple and people came here to forget about the outside world for a few hours.

The fact that his experiences within the community for the past year or so had been soothing his soul less and less wasn't the fault of the people. In fact, one of the only reasons he still came to the Citadel was because there were good friends inside. Friends who had made the whole process of relocating back to Dallas more bearable.

"Good evening, sir."

"Good evening, Henry. How are you?"

The submissive's radiant smile illuminated the dark entryway and his effervescent personality made him perfect for the position of welcome boy.

"I'm great. Master Everett and I are doing a caning demonstration this evening in the main playroom."

"I'll look forward to observing. You are always beautiful in your submission. Master Everett is a very lucky man."

The young man practically glowed at the mention of his Dominant's name. Everett and Henry had recently signed a permanent contract, after having been together for nearly two years. Aside from Brandon and Tyler, the two men were the closest friends Javier had. Therefore, he wasn't going to rain on Henry's parade and tell him that the thought of watching him get caned would be the last thing he wanted to end his day.

Everett was the owner of the Citadel and one of the best Dominants Javier had the pleasure of knowing. But he was so much more than a leader in the BDSM community. He was a brilliant businessman, and with every look between the two of them, it was clear Everett thought the world revolved around Henry.

It had, in fact, been Everett who'd introduced Javier to his last sub. Unfortunately, things had not worked out between him and Vincent. A couple of months ago, Javier had made the decision to end their association.

At first, Vincent had seemed a model sub, but a little over a month into their relationship, something had shifted in their dynamic. At first, it had been as subtle as a sneer in the mirror. A tightening of muscles at even a casual touch. It had been during one particular scene at his home that Javier had felt a quiver of animosity come from Vincent. He'd immediately called a stop and initiated a discussion about what was going on in the sub's head. His sub's state of mind and care during a scene were always his first responsibilities. But despite his best efforts to understand what Vincent needed, Javier had never felt they'd been able to forge a foundation to build on. So now he found himself without a submissive and, lately, questioning why he wasn't actively searching for one.

He still enjoyed coming to the Citadel. Sharing space and socializing with like-minded individuals relaxed him in a way that a local mainstream bar never did. And today just happened to be one of those that he needed his friends. All day long he'd been putting out one fire after another.

Ninety percent of the time, he loved working with the patients at the sports and spine rehabilitation center where he was the chief physical therapist. But ten percent of the time he encountered a combination of either patients or management duties that sucked a piece of his soul. Right now, he was running on fumes.

He stepped through the interior doors and took in the scene. It was still early for a Thursday night, but there were a few members relaxing on the sofas and deep chairs scattered around the room. Walking up to the bar, he saw Everett playing bartender.

"Rough day?"

He nodded. "Can I get a shot of Maestro?"

Everett paused. "You know the rules."

"I'm just here to relax tonight. You know what? Make it a double."

Everett slid the shot towards Javier. "What's going on?"

"I had a client call just before leaving work. I've been helping him rehab for the last several months after a spinal fusion surgery. But he wanted to let me know that he couldn't make his appointment in the morning. Apparently his wife, who's been battling cancer, is being moved into a hospice."

"That sucks."

Javier nodded. "I know I'm not a licensed counselor, but we've spent many of our hours together talking about his ailing spouse. I feel as though I've gotten to know her in a way." He swallowed the shot. "You should have heard his voice. If heartbreak has a sound, it echoed through that phone line into my ear. They never had any children, and neither of them have any living siblings. Only each other, and it seems like that's soon going to change."

"That's rough, man, but I get the feeling there's more. You're not the overly emotional type. So why the double shot?"

He looked around the room. Everyone present was paired up, and in the last several months he'd gotten to know the regular members well enough that he recognized the majority of them. Committed. Devoted. Each and every one. But maybe there were some people who simply didn't have it in them to experience love like his client. Like Everett and Henry. If he were being honest, he knew more people who'd had a series of failed relationships than those who were successful. Sometimes even love wasn't enough. *Take my parents, for instance.*

His mother had devoted her whole life to Javier's father. But one day he'd woken up and simply said, *'I don't love you anymore. I'm not even sure I ever did.'* Next thing Javier knew, he and his *madre* had been living with his *abuelos*. And the woman who'd been raised from birth to be a wife and mother had had to go out and find work. With little education and no experience, the best she'd been able to manage was a night shift job in a warehouse. Which meant every morning while he ate his breakfast, he got to hear how his *madre* had failed. How if she had just kept her faith in Christ and been the woman his father needed, then he would never have questioned his devotion.

Then there was Brandon and Tyler. Anyone with at least one eye could see that those two men loved each other. They were exactly what the other needed, but miscommunication, fears and sheer stubbornness had had them on the outs for the last month.

"Guess the whole conversation really made me think about relationships. Why some work and others don't. Why even when it seems like two people are a perfect match, everything still manages to go wrong."

"Is this about Vincent? I'm sorry. I really thought the two of you would be good together."

He eyed the bottle still sitting on the bar but knew another shot wasn't a good idea.

Maybe a beer instead?

"Not your fault." He pasted on a smile. "Hey, we can't all be as lucky as you. Henry is special and his devotion to you is unparalleled."

Everett looked towards the door and the warmth and heat in his eyes at making eye contact with his sub made Javier feel as though he was interrupting an intimate moment.

"Yes, he is. But it also took me many years to find him. I know you'll find the man who's right for you, too."

There was a shift in the air pressure and Javier turned towards the door. He sucked in a hard breath as the sight of Vincent entering the club. Physically he was exactly what Javier gravitated towards — an imposing man with large muscles, a bald head and bright blue eyes. Right now, he vibrated with an energy that had Javier frowning. Vincent glanced around the room as if he was looking for someone.

Vincent hadn't been back to the club in the two months since their separation. Javier had offered to help the man find a new Dominant, but Vincent had said he needed some time to process what had happened between them before starting over. Was he here now because he was ready?

Well, the least I can do is introduce him to a few of the Doms. I'll leave it up to him to figure out who'll be the best fit, since clearly I never figured it out.

Javier realized he was sitting in the shadow of a pillar. He moved to stand and as soon as Vincent saw him, his entire demeanor changed. It was as if he'd pulled a cloak over himself to portray a part.

"Are you sure this is the wisest course of action?" Everett asked softly.

"No, but I owe it to him. I may have failed him, but he's still my responsibility in a way until he finds another Dom."

"I'm here if you need anything."

Javier turned towards Everett. "*Lo se, mi amigo.*"

He started toward Vincent. It only took a dozen or so steps but felt much farther. Even though his and Vincent's arrangement hadn't worked out, he shouldn't feel this anxiety about approaching a submissive. What did that say about him as a Dom? Maybe, after tonight, he would reevaluate his ideals. When he'd first admitted he was gay, he'd gotten so hung up on being seen as a man of strength that he'd instantly gravitated towards a relationship that required a power dynamic. That had actually led to a truly unhealthy relationship with Tyler one summer. In his anger and self-hatred, he'd treated Tyler cruelly. A few years later, Javier had come back to Dallas with a new perspective.

He was fortunate that Tyler had forgiven him and the two of them now shared a friendship of mutual respect. But maybe it was time to take another look within and decide if being a Dom was his true calling. Maybe it wasn't only Vincent's fault that their relationship hadn't worked. Maybe Javier was to blame as well. If his heart wasn't in building a dynamic, then how could he ever expect one to develop?

"Vincent. Please join me." Javier gestured towards two chairs nearby.

He expected Vincent to follow behind him as a sub typically did, but instead the man almost brushed past. Javier stopped walking and Vincent took two more steps before halting and looking back.

"Apologies, Master."

Javier shook his head. "My name is Javier or Sir, if you still feel the need. I believe the title of Master is a moniker only appropriate when a permanent contract between Dom and sub has been agreed upon." He continued toward the chairs and when Vincent moved to kneel, Javier stopped him. "The chair, please."

Vincent frowned. "Sir?"

Javier sat and relaxed against the cushions. He didn't want Vincent to sense the tension radiating throughout his body. "My expectations of you are different now that we're no longer together."

"That's what I wanted to talk to you about. I'd really like to come back. I've missed you, Sir."

Javier take a closer look at the man. "That surprises me. For weeks leading up to our separation, I sensed your dissatisfaction in our relationship."

"You could tell that?"

"Part of being a good Dominant is the ability to read micro-expressions and body language from a sub. You said the right words, but I could tell your heart and mind weren't engaged. Trust is a fundamental in our community and you didn't trust me." He sighed. "And I've come to realize that I didn't trust you either."

He studied the man across from him. He wore a placid mask, but his fingers clutched his beefy thighs.

"I've had a rough couple of months at work. My head wasn't in the game before, but things are better now. I can try harder—"

Javier held up his hand. "I don't think that's the problem. You recently moved to Dallas, and, believe me, I know the stress of relocation and starting over. But here's the question I've asked myself. If the arrangement between us was right, then it should have been a time of peace. A time of clarity. Instead, when we were together, I perceived a wall between us, and despite my best efforts, the mortar only grew stronger. So, it became clear that we weren't the right match."

"I think you're wrong, but I suppose there's nothing I can do to change your mind. How about one last scene as a goodbye? We can even go back to your place, so there's no public talk about us together again."

Javier frowned. "That's not really appropriate, but I will agree to a final drink. You said you needed time before you were ready to search out a new Dom. I'm still willing to help you with that, if you wish. If possible, I'd like to remain friends."

"Thank you, Sir. Sorry, Javier. Can we maybe have the drink somewhere else?" Vincent looked around the room. "I don't really feel like being here right now."

Vincent locked eyes with someone in the direction of the bar. Javier assumed Everett was watching over them. Everett had a perfect resting Dom face, as Javier liked to joke. If that look was focused on Vincent at the moment, no wonder the man was squirming in his seat a bit. Javier was really tempted to look over his shoulder, but he refused to satisfy his curiosity. "Of course. Where would you like to go?"

"I know a little friendly place not far from here."

"Sounds good. I'll meet you there."

"Actually, the parking is the one drawback. Not a big lot. We can ride together, and I'll bring you back or I can ride with you."

Javier nodded. "Let me just clear it with Everett that I can leave my car here for a little while."

Javier looked over at the bar, but Everett had disappeared and the usual bartender was in his place. His friend was probably in his office, doing administration stuff. He didn't really think it would be a big deal to leave his car on the premises for an hour or so. He sent a text instead and nodded at Vincent.

Maybe what I've been missing since breaking it off with Vincent is closure? Maybe now I'll find the drive to find someone new?

And maybe that someone new didn't have to be a trained submissive. If he opened his mind and heart to all possibilities instead of trying to fit a relationship into a pre-formed mold, then was it possible to finally find the right person?

"Let's go." They left though the front doors and as they passed Henry, Javier nodded. "I'll be back. Please inform your Master I'd like to speak with him when I do."

"Yes, Sir."

The fresh air hit Javier the moment they exited the building. A breeze caressed his face with enough energy to dissipate the lingering warmth of the day. It also helped that the sun was no longer doing its best to blind them from the sky.

"I'm parked over here," Vincent said.

Javier turned the corner of the building and followed Vincent toward the parking lot in back. He saw Vincent's truck right away. The bright white late model Ford stuck out in the sea of darker vehicles. Not to mention the blue lights that flashed brightly as he unlocked the doors, momentarily blinding Javier. He'd actually always hated the vehicle.

He climbed in on the passenger side and put on his seatbelt. He sniffed and detected the scent of a cheap air freshener that maybe should have been refreshing, but really resembled Pine-Sol mixed with spearmint. As soon as Vincent started the engine, he lowered the window a few inches. One drink or two as a courtesy, then it was back to the Citadel.

He watched the buildings of the Deep Ellum neighborhood pass by. Lights from other clubs and restaurants blurred together as they drove. He sat up as he realized that Vincent was driving south, away from the entertainment district.

"Just where are we going?"

"Someplace you'll never forget."

Vincent's voice sounded different. Javier turned and found himself staring at the end of a Taser.

"Hey —"

Javier jerked when Vincent pulled the trigger. Every muscle in his body contracted and his throat burned with the scream he unleashed before blackness enveloped him.

Chapter One

May 2017
Seven months later

Javier groaned. It felt like Bobby Lashley had body-slammed him on the pavement over and over again. He tried to get his brain to follow his command to open his eyes. He was in his cell again, lying on his side in the fetal position, nipples on fire, testicles nowhere to be found, soaking wet, with his left arm tucked under his body in the oddest position.

He took inventory of his latest injuries. A trickle of something dripping down his back told him his latest lacerations were still bleeding, so he probably hadn't been unconscious for very long. The ever-present abrasions on his wrists and ankles appeared a shade darker than the last time he'd looked. There were new burn marks on his torso too. His body shivered with a concerning combination of heat and cold. His training told him that he was probably fighting some kind of infection. Bacterial was most likely, due to the many untreated burns and lacerations he'd sustained since getting in that fucking truck with Vincent.

How much time had gone since he'd passed out in Vincent's torture room? His cell had no windows — in fact, Javier hadn't seen any sign of outdoors since the moment he'd woken up in his new hell. He couldn't even use the length of his hair or beard to tell time because Vincent never allowed it to grow. He'd wake up, hungover from whatever drug Vincent had injected him with that time, to feel his face and head completely shaved. Combine that with the blank spots in his memories, and for all he knew he could be an old man by now. He certainly felt like it.

The only way he'd managed to retain his sanity was by using his training to keep his mind focused on something other than the pain, by cataloging each muscle group and bone being tortured by his kidnapper at any given time. More than once he'd popped his shoulder back into its socket. Based on the intermittent swelling, loss of range of motion and instability of his left leg he suspected an ACL injury.

How much longer could he tolerate these *scenes*, as Vincent called them? The man was a fucking psychopath — or, actually, sociopath would probably be a better diagnosis. He'd somehow managed to convince everyone in Javier's circle that he was a trained submissive, even passed all the background checks for the club membership. But clearly it had all been a façade. A very cleverly crafted and multilayered portrayal. *The man should get the fucking Oscar of all Oscars then get taken right to the goddamn electric chair.*

Javier rolled onto his hands and knees, but collapsed onto his elbows. The splotch of dirt on the floor spun in circles beneath his nose. If his protruding ribcage was an indication, he'd dropped significant weight and muscle mass, but his stomach no longer told him if he was hungry. He pushed up again and raised his head a few inches. A few feet away was the sagging excuse for a mattress that inhabited the corner of his cell. He started to crawl, but the pressure on his knee was too great. Javier took a deep breath and walked his hands up the wall till he was mostly vertical. The cement felt cool on his skin and he sighed in pleasure till his back made contact and lighting bolts of pain ricocheted through his body.

"*Me cago en la hostia de tu puta madre.*"

"Now, now. My mother never did anything to you."

Javier whipped around and was immediately hit with a wave of vertigo. He tried to fixate on Vincent to stop the spinning, but the giant ogre's face just got uglier with the tilt-a-whirl in Javier's head.

"You look a little worse for wear. I brought you some food. You really did beautifully that last session, so I thought some nourishment would be a nice reward."

Javier gathered what saliva he had in his mouth and spat. There was a flash of movement then his head was filled with sound of a thousand gongs, and his right cheekbone throbbed from the impact of the food tray.

"You fucking ungrateful spic!"

Vincent was turning a concerning shade of red. It wasn't the first time his captor had lost his composure. Javier had fought both physically and mentally against Vincent from the moment he'd became conscious, trapped inside a black hood. But he'd never seen the veins on the side of Vincent's shaved head pop out quite that dramatically.

"I think it's time for the next phase of your training. I've been understanding up till now. I know that submission doesn't come naturally to you, but, you see, even the toughest of the tough can be broken." Vincent pulled Javier in so their noses touched. "I know, because I've broken them. And I will break you all eventually."

"Why? What the fuck is all this for? I never mistreated you. Hell, I'd never even met you before Everett introduced us."

"*Tsk, tsk.* How many times do we need to have this conversation? Maybe I need to lay off the breath control if it's affecting your memory. Hypoxia...such a tricky thing to get right," Vincent said, smiling.

He was fucking sure Vincent had never told him what his motives were. Well, maybe ninety percent sure. Vincent pushed him away and Javier stumbled, tripping on the edge of his mattress and falling to the musky surface.

"Eat up! Phase two of your training will begin shortly," Vincent said as he walked out of the room.

He had to figure a way to secure his release. Clearly nobody was coming for him. Hell, he didn't even know if anyone had figured out he'd been taken. When he counted the number of close acquaintances in his life, it was pathetically low. And everyone was so tied up in their own lives that it wasn't unreasonable to assume nobody was screaming at the cops that something was wrong.

He scooped up the piece of bread and chunks of cheese that Vincent had brought him. If he was going to fight for his life, he needed fuel. But how was he going to escape? He'd never seen the walls outside this room. Anytime Vincent took him somewhere else, he was hooded. In the space Vincent called his playroom, Javier was always blindfolded. He knew there were no stairs between rooms, but the space didn't feel like a home. It was cold. He'd never encountered a soft surface. The air had a staleness about it. On the other hand, the spaces didn't have a large feel to them, like an industrial or warehouse setting. The first thing he had to do was figure out the layout of the building. It wouldn't do him any good to start stumbling around blindly. That was assuming he found a way to break free of Vincent in the first place.

* * * *

Ten…eleven…twelve…

"Here we are. Time for your shower. As much as I enjoy working with you, I have no desire to wear a nose plug due to your stench."

Vincent gave Javier a little push. He felt tile beneath his bare feet. He stretched his arms out and turned, trying to get an impression of the space. He cried out when Vincent yanked him backwards by the ties of the blindfold. He squinted as the blackness disappeared. His eyes burned from the bright light, but Javier noticed he was still partially standing out in the hallway. He quickly assessed as much as he could before Vincent pushed him into the bathroom and slammed the door shut.

"Don't think to try anything funny. I've removed any tools or items that could benefit you in any other way than to clean the stink. You have five minutes."

This was a new room. Javier's standard 'bathroom' was a bucket and bathing was no more than a quick dousing of liquid soap then spray from a garden hose in the corner of his cell. Why would Vincent give him access to a real bathroom at this point? Javier assumed it was because Vincent's favorite form of tormenting him was to play up uncertainty. There was never a schedule or pattern to when things happened, or even where. Sometimes Vincent would take him to the playroom and other times he would torture him right there in his cell, to ensure that Javier had no safe space.

The bathroom was utilitarian for sure, but he now knew that this room was twelve steps to the right of the playroom. Since he'd made the decision to start mapping his surroundings, he'd learned that his cell was twenty steps to the left away from the playroom. That one had taken some extra time and math because sometimes he'd been unconscious when leaving the playroom, but come to partway back. Other times Vincent would inject him with a sedative before they left and he wouldn't wake up till he was strapped onto one of the pieces of bondage equipment.

He'd yet to encounter any corners during his mental mapping. So that would indicate at least this part of the building was one long hallway. There had to be other doors, though, and logically an exit someplace. Those were thoughts for another time. There was only a wall sink, toilet and small shower stall. No mirror to break, curtain or glass door on the shower to use as a weapon. No knickknacks to use as missiles. Hell, there wasn't even a plunger he could use to beat the shit *into* Vincent. There was, however, a commercial grade paper towel holder. A bit vague, but a clue about his location nonetheless. He took a look inside.

Just the thing I need.

He turned on the shower just in case Vincent was listening on the other side of the door. He even stepped into the stall and checked the visible areas for cameras. He couldn't lose the element of surprise. The water splashing at his feet was so very tempting, but being free was infinitely better than being clean. It looked like the room was clear of any surveillance. At least as far as he could tell. He would just have to risk it.

Javier retrieved the liner that was sitting on the bottom of the mini trashcan attached to the paper towel holder. For good measure he squeezed a giant blob of shampoo into the liner and tried to mush it around.

Now where to wait for my prey?

Behind the door seemed the most logical place, but he didn't want to trap himself.

"One minute!" Vincent yelled through the door

Javier closed his eyes, said the fastest prayer in history and let out a long breath. He shut out the lights and stood in the corner on the opposite side of the door. Everything hurt and he sincerely hoped his body still had the strength to pull this off.

The door banged open and Javier struck. He jumped and covered Vincent's head with the trash bag liner.

"Motherfucker!" Vincent screamed through the bag. "You're going to die even slower for this!"

The threat only made Javier grip tighter. Vincent spun and Javier's back slammed into the wall where the towel holder was attached. A rib definitely snapped and he almost lost his grip, but Javier put his feet against the wall and pushed with everything he had. They flew across the room and Vincent's head slammed into the tile wall. They crashed to the floor in a tangle of limbs. Vincent tried to stab his fingers into the thin plastic covering his mouth.

No!

Javier drew on his last reserves of adrenaline to roll them so that Vincent was face-planted on the floor. Vincent tried to push up, but Javier kneed him in the kidneys and tightened the bag incrementally more. The other man was bigger, stronger, healthier, but Javier had pure rage on his side. He was going to get the fuck out of here. He was not going to let himself be a victim anymore.

The sound of water pounding on the tile mixed with their screams. The floor started to get wet, and Javier slipped. He didn't dare look up at the shower head. He'd seen too many movies where the good guy was just about to win and got distracted, only to have his ass handed to him.

Javier gave Vincent several more sharp jabs with his knees, striking wherever he could reach. With each hit his damaged knee throbbed so much that it felt as though the insides were about to explode. Vincent tried to grab at the back of the bag, but a quick slam of his head onto the tile floor stopped that effort.

How fucking long does it take to make the guy go unconscious?

Vincent suddenly went slack, but Javier wasn't about to fall for the abrupt change. He knew that suffocation was a slow process, not something that happened from one second to the next. He kept hold of the bag and angled his head to the side of Vincent's, placing his mouth near Vincent's ear.

"Not falling for it, asshole," he growled.

Vincent heaved and tried to flip Javier off his body, but the lack of oxygen had weakened him.

Just a little longer. I've got to hold on just another minute or so.

Javier's arms screamed with fatigue. He had a hard time drawing a deep breath. Suddenly a lightning bolt of pain speared through his right quad. He fell against Vincent, driving the knife that his captor had somehow managed to stab him with deeper till he swore the tip glanced off his bone.

"*Gilipollas!*"

Tears streaked down Javier's face. His fingers started to go numb and snot dripped from his nose. But with every second, Vincent's air supply became smaller. The man's muscles started to spasm, a sign hypoxia was finally setting in.

The thrashing, screaming body beneath him slowed. Vincent's curses stopped pummeling Javier's ears. With every jerk of their bodies, the knife in Javier's leg shifted, rending more muscle tissue. The floor was slick, but Javier dug his toes into the grout for traction. At last a blanket of stillness finally settled over Vincent.

Javier tried to catch his breath as he finally lost the battle to hold back his tears. He reached and used the sink to pull himself up, favoring his right leg. Blindly groping for the wall, Javier tried to find the light switch. He found the door handle first and jerked it open. Light from the hall spilled into the small room, highlighting Vincent's body on the water- and blood-soaked floor. The plastic bag concealed the face of his torturer, but the man's image was burned into Javier's mind forever. He forced his eyes away from the scene to look down and saw the knife protruding from his leg.

He knew he couldn't run looking like a stuck pig, and he had to get out of there. He gripped the hilt of the dagger.

"Really hope I'm not about to bleed out."

He pulled, biting his lip so hard he tasted blood, to avoid screaming. The blade came free and there was no indication that an artery was compromised. He did need to stop the residual bleeding somehow. A few shuffled steps back into the bathroom and Javier leaned over Vincent. He used the knife to slice a strip of cloth from the man's shirt.

He stared down at his unconscious kidnapper. The man wasn't dead yet, but Javier gripped the knife tighter, knowing he could make it so if he had the fortitude to take a life. His body hurt, his heart hurt. Trails of blood tickled his leg, waking him from his stupor.

He fell to his knees, raised the dagger high over his head and closed his eyes. He could hear his abuela's voice in his head.

Piensa de nuevo en lo que Dios quiere que creas. Y en lo que quiereque hagas.

Vincent moaned and Javier's eyes flew open. His fears of what God may have wanted him to believe or do became irrelevant to survival. He plunged the knife down into the back of Vincent's head. When it stopped moving, Javier promptly vomited. Bile burned his esophagus as tears and snot dripped down his face. Skittering, he didn't stop till his back reached the wall of the hallway.

"Get up, Javier. Get up. Get up!"

He quickly wrapped the strip of cloth, that he'd somehow managed to hold on to, around his leg and tied it tightly. Bracing his back against the wall, he levered himself into a standing position. His head felt like a lead balloon perched on top of his neck, but he managed to look away from the dead body. He blinked several times, trying to focus on the immediate situation. He had to get the fuck out of Dodge.

This was his first real look at his environment. It was indeed a hallway. He had two choices, but for the life of him he couldn't remember which direction they'd come from. He turned right, and after about twelve steps found himself outside a door. He could open it and see for himself the room where Vincent had done his best to break him, or he could move on to his future.

Javier kept walking. He saw an end to the hallway just a handful of steps away. He paused and peered around the corner. The space opened up into a barn-like structure. A quick sniff carried a hint of stale fertilizer in the air. Rows of wooden tables and scattered shelving indicated that this had been at one point a nursery. He saw a pair of glass doors, covered in brown paper. Javier stumbled his way over, his leg seconds away from giving out just as he pressed his hands against the metal frame of the door.

The doors rattled as he pushed, but did not open. "No!" The deadbolt of the door was just visible between the metal frames. The most likely answer was that Vincent kept the keys either on him or stashed somewhere, but fuck if he was going on a treasure hunt. He examined the area, looking for something he could use to break the glass. A rock, an old flower pot — hell, he was even ready to kung fu one of the tables and grab a piece of wood.

"Or I could just look for another door."

Nope. He was getting out this way or not at all, and option two wasn't acceptable. He could risk taking a running leap to break through, but his catalog of injuries was high enough already. He looked down and, as he bent to start searching the ground, he felt a draft over his back. He turned and out of the corner of his eye saw a sheet of plastic beneath one of the tables on the other side of the room. He tried to stand, but his body refused to listen to his brain.

Crawling his way across the room, slower than he probably had done as a baby, he stared at the plastic, making sure it wasn't an apparition of some kind, mentally pleading that it really was a way out and not just taunting him with the possibility. He reached out and his fingers brushed the opaque barrier.

"Please, please," he whispered.

He pushed the plastic to the side and tears slid down his face when the fresh air of the outside world hit him. His left hand encountered dirt as he crawled through, and Javier dug his fingers into the loose soil. He made it through and looked around. There were a couple of long red metal buildings and some half-moon greenhouses, but an air of desolation permeated the air. The business must have closed a while ago, but Javier didn't recognize it. He heard road noise coming from not far away. There was nothing but a sea of dead fields in front of him. Foot by foot he worked his way around the building. As he turned the final corner, he saw a large empty gravel parking lot with a sliding chain-link gate.

That empty parking lot was a white desert standing between him and the promise of a lifesaving oasis. He took his first step and the rock bit into the soles of his bare feet. The flares of pain were more of a nuisance than problematic. Javier gripped the fence. He didn't have the strength to climb over.

The sound of an engine came from his left. The brightness of the sun made the truck's image waver like a mirage.

"Help!" he cried, waving his arm.

The truck sped past and Javier really didn't think he had anything left. He found himself unable to stand any longer. His head jerked up at the sound of screeching brakes. The truck skidded to a stop, and Javier gipped the metal rings of the fence till his fingers went white.

"Help," he cried, weakly.

A man came running towards him, and Javier tried to reach through the fence.

"Holy shit, man. Are you okay?"

He couldn't find any words. He just let emotions have free rein, and prayed his savior understood him.

"I have a pair of bolt cutters in my truck. I'll be right back. Um, I should ask, are you alone?"

Was he alone? He was more alone than this stranger could even understand.

"I'll be right back. I promise. I'm going to get you out."

The words were a pledge, but Javier had a feeling that getting out was only the beginning.

Chapter Two

He opened his eyes slowly, but the world was out of focus. Javier blinked several times and slowly the blur faded.

"Hey, you're awake!"

It was a chore getting his head to turn towards the voice. He couldn't seem to stop the tears from welling up when Brandon and Tyler appeared beside the hospital bed. One or both of them had been there every time he'd opened his eyes for the past several days.

Brandon stood quickly. "Don't worry, it's going to be okay."

They'd been pumping antibiotics through his veins to fight off the sepsis, and he still felt like hammered shit. He couldn't seem to find his voice, and when he tried to shake his head, it felt like a thousand marbles were smashing against one another.

Tyler gripped Javier's hand. "Look, I know you're still not completely with it, but the cops have been in and out, trying to talk to you. I managed to overhear a few words here and there, and…did you do it?"

Javier nodded. He'd done it. He'd killed a man. Granted, Vincent had probably only been buying time before *he* did the deed, but clearly Javier wasn't the badass he'd always imagined himself to be, given that he'd been on the verge of tears from the moment he'd woken up in the hospital.

"Good," Brandon and Tyler said together.

"Look, the cops are going to be back soon to ask questions. Do you want to talk to them or you want me to tell them to fuck off?" Brandon asked.

Javier tried to grin, but winced when his lip split. "It has to be done. I was looking forward to going home, but guess it's off to another prison for me."

Tyler gripped Javier's hand harder. "Bullshit. It was self-defense. Any idiot can understand that. The fucker kidnapped and tortured you for seven goddamn months."

Even though he was lying down, his head started to spin. "What?"

"What, what? I get that you're probably not thinking very clearly yet, but even you have to admit your logic doesn't hold up. How many people get sent to jail for defending their lives?"

He couldn't seem to catch his breath and there was a loud beeping sound assaulting his ears.

"What's going on in here?" a nurse said, running into the room. He placed one hand on Javier's abdomen, just below his ribs, and the other on his chest. "Mr. Alde, you need to breathe in through your nose and out through your mouth."

He tried to follow the nurse's directions, but his vision started to go black around the edges.

"What's wrong?" Brandon asked.

"Again, Mr. Alde. Come on, you can do it. Move my hands with the air coming in and going out. Focus on each breath. I can get a sedative if I have to."

That was enough of a threat that he tried to focus and stop himself from hyperventilating. Gradually the black faded and his chest didn't feel as if it were being crushed. The loud beeping went away, and awareness crept in that the nurse had been notified his heart monitor was going berserk.

"That's better. Now, was it something medical that triggered the panic attack?"

"No, I'm sor—"

"Hey, none of that. You're going through a lot of shit right now, pardon the unprofessional language. So no apologies for having a freak-out moment. In fact, I'm amazed this was your first one. I just need to make sure it wasn't triggered by something medical."

"Seven months?" Javier asked, his voice cracking.

The nurse looked across at Brandon and Tyler and Javier turned his head, seeking out his best friends. He must have heard them wrong.

Tyler sighed and sank into the chair near the window. "Yeah. I thought you knew that. Fuck, I'm sorry, man."

Brandon sat on the arm of the chair and ran his hand over the back of Tyler's head. Now that Javier really looked, there was something different about the two of them. Gone was the thin transparent wall separating them from one another. Brandon had always been somewhat aloof and snarky, but now his eyes and touch on his lover radiated concern and support.

"Apparently, you're not the only one who needs to be interrogated. All right, give us your best shot."

Ah, there's the snark.

"Honestly, I'm not even really sure if I know what I don't know."

"Gentlemen, sounds like you have things under control here. I'm going back on rounds. Hit the Call button if you need anything." Frowning, the nurse left the room.

"Um, let's start with what's his name again?"

Tyler pointed to the dry erase board. "Day nurse is Keith. Night nurse is Angela."

"Right. My memory is for shit right now. So seven months. That means it's…"

"May 2017. You missed an awesome New Year's Eve party. It was a total rager."

Javier smirked at the absurdity of Brandon's last statement, despite the fact that his gut clenched at having lost so much time. How had he not somehow subconsciously realized that two entire seasons had passed while he was locked away?

"You're in Lubbock at University Medical Center."

"Yeah, that one I got, based on all the signage around here. I assume, judging by what I see in front of me, that Brandon stopped being a paranoid control freak and the two of you are good?"

"I know you're all busted up, so I won't ever so politely say 'Go fuck yourself'."

There was no heat in the words, and Javier found himself smiling, despite everything but his mouth hurting.

Tyler took Brandon's hand and pulled the man over for a kiss. "I love you, but you can be such a dick."

Brandon smiled at Tyler. "Well, at least I'm not an asshole." He looked over at Javier. "In all seriousness, we're good. Believe it or not, I'm a cowboy now!"

Javier squinted and tried to give Brandon a look of disbelief but feared, with his face looking the way it did, he didn't quite pull it off. "Somehow I can't exactly picture you out in a barn shoveling shit."

"Meh, once you've seen your boyfriend's arm up a horse's va-jay-jay, you're only half a step away from living a real-life *True Grit* adventure."

Tyler rolled his eyes. "Don't listen to him."

"Oh, I never do."

Brandon growled and Javier realized exactly what his friends were up to. It would be so easy for him to lie in this bed and fall apart, but Brandon and Tyler were doing everything in their power to make him feel as if they were sitting in a bar, having drinks on the weekend. All three of them were doing a damn good job of hiding behind the masks of normalcy. But the veneer was thin. Brandon had dark circles under his eyes and Tyler's hair stuck up in ten different directions. The signs of his ordeal were written over every inch of Javier's body. So, as much as he appreciated the effort, the problem was that he wasn't normal anymore.

"Javier Alde?"

He turned and was met with just one more reminder of the recent events. The door to his hospital room was filled by two men flashing badges and wearing stern expressions.

"Yes?"

"My name is Detective Berberidis and this is Detective Kirner. We need to speak to you."

Javier nodded. "I understand."

Detective Kirner looked over at Tyler and Brandon. "Can you please step out?"

Brandon stood, folding his arms. "Is this an interrogation? Due to his extreme injuries, Mr. Alde has not had the opportunity to contact his attorney yet." He took out his cell. "I believe he has that right before he says anything to you. I'll be happy to call him and you gentleman can return at a later time with notice."

God bless Brandon, but Javier knew putting off the discussion or interrogation wasn't going to change the facts.

"It's okay. I'll talk to them."

Tyler stood. "I understand where you are coming from, Javier, but I've been in business long enough to say with authority that having a lawyer present is never a bad idea." He directed his stare at the detective. "Even when a person is completely innocent."

Detective Berberidis sighed. "Gentlemen, I understand you're trying to protect your friend's interests, but technically, if you don't allow us to speak to him, that's impeding an investigation. This is not an interrogation. Mr. Alde is not being charged with anything at this time. We are simply trying to gather all the facts of the case."

"I'll agree to talk to you, if my friends can remain present."

The two detectives looked at each other and shrugged. "Fine with us for now."

Brandon tapped the screen of his phone. "I'll record the conversation. Just so there's no confusion later."

Detective Kirner took out a small notebook. "Can you please tell us about how you knew Mr. Pesano?"

Javier frowned. "I'm sorry, who?"

Berberidis squinted and tensed his jaw. "The man we found with a knife in the back of his skull inside a bathroom of a vacated nursery. The same vacated nursery you were found running from by a passing motorist."

"His name is, sorry was, Vincent Finch. Not Pesano."

Kirner looked down at his notebook. "His fingerprints matched those of a Mr. Luca Pesano from Long Island, New York."

Javier shook his head. "I don't know anything about that. I met Vincent last June. We were introduced by a mutual friend and started dating. Our relationship didn't develop the way I had hoped, and I broke it off with him in August. I didn't see him again until the beginning of October when we ran into each other at a club. That night he asked to go out for a drink. I saw it as a way to get closure, so I agreed. I made the mistake of getting in his car and it was then he hit me with a Taser. I have no recollection of getting from Dallas to the location from where I escaped. He kept me prisoner and tortured me in ways I will not speak of at this time. Two days ago, I saw an opportunity to escape, and I did. When I made it out of the building, I flagged down a passing truck and must have passed out. Because I woke up here."

"And your opportunity to 'escape' just happens to involve killing a man? It's a tad convenient that he can't tell his side of the story, don't you think? How do we know that he abducted you at all? How do we know that the two of you didn't just get into a fight? It's not like you tried to hide the evidence. The knife was still sticking out of his head, and your fingerprints were all over the handle."

Javier's heart raced in his chest. For a moment he thought he could still smell the odor of his vomit mixed with the blood on the floor of that bathroom. He vaguely heard Brandon's and Tyler's voices mixing with those of the detectives'.

"Mr. Alde!"

"It was me or him. I had no choice! If you check...if you check the knife, you should also find his prints. And my blood. You guys can do that, right? Or do all those cop shows lie about the forensic two-donor stuff?" He whipped the sheet away from the lower half of his body and pulled down his hospital gown to expose his chest. "He stabbed me in the leg while I was trying to get away." He held out his arms. "Look at me! Do you think all these injuries happened in a single fight?"

Detective Kirner held up his hand. "I hear you. And we are in the processes of examining all the evidence. Including the *entire* building."

They'd found the other rooms. Javier tried to blink away the evidence of the wave of humiliation that swamped him.

"There is one thing I'm struggling to understand. You're claiming that you were in that building for the past seven months, against your will, and nobody reported you missing?"

"I did!" Brandon shouted. "When I hadn't heard anything from him in a couple of weeks, I went to his apartment, his work and I checked his social media accounts. He'd disappeared. I filed a missing person's report with the Dallas Police. They said there was nothing they could do because there were no signs of any suspicious activity. His work had received a notice of resignation, his landlord was told Javier was breaking the lease, all his accounts had been closed. They said he must have just decided to leave. But I knew it was bullshit."

"Why?"

"One, Javier had just moved to Dallas a year before that. Two, he loved his job and would never quit, especially without notice. And three, he was so proud of his fancy apartment you'd think the address was 1600 Pennsylvania Avenue."

Tyler stood. "I too spoke with Detective Mercer with the Dallas Police Department. I explained that I had reservations about Vincent based on some behaviors I'd observed that summer when they were still together."

"What behaviors would that be?"

"I know this is strictly anecdotal, but it was the way he looked at Javier when his back was turned. Almost like he was playing a part. One minute he'd be..." Tyler looked at Javier for a second. "Acting as a typical new lover, but the next there was this manic hatred in his eyes, then flash and back to before. However, we only met him one time. And, unfortunately, it was at a graduation party for a friend, so the evening was quite chaotic. Hardly the place for an intimate conversation, getting to know someone. My gut wasn't much for Detective Mercer to go on, and I was told when he did a quick background check nothing was red-flagged. We reached out to Javier's friend who introduced them for more information, but that didn't lead anywhere."

"Why not?" Kirner asked.

"Everett only knew what personal information was listed on Vincent's application. And all member information is held strictly confidential. He wouldn't be able to tell Tyler and Brandon anything, even if he wanted to." Javier looked at his friends. "Thank you. I had no idea you both tried so hard. Why didn't you say anything to me about your suspicions?"

Tyler griped the rails of Javier's bed. "Of course we tried. You're our friend. You have no idea how guilty I feel about that in hindsight. But you'd broken it off with him, and we had no reason to think you were still in contact."

"Back up a second." Berberidis said. "What do you mean application and member information?"

Javier inhaled, slowly. His ribs still reminded him with every breath how being tossed against a paper towel dispenser had not been a good idea.

"I suppose it's going to come out sooner or later. Vincent and I were members of the Citadel. That's how we met. We were introduced by the owner Everett Pearson. He thought the two of us would be a good match."

"The what? Is this some kind of dating site?" Berberidis asked.

Javier saw a flash of recognition in Kirner's eyes, but the man stayed quiet.

"It's an exclusive club in Dallas."

"I suppose this has something to do with you being a homosexual?"

"While I don't deny that I'm gay, the club is open to individuals of all genders and orientations."

"So what makes it so exclusive? Why the secret identity of its members?"

He had a feeling this whole conversation was about to take a turn. He looked at Tyler, trying to judge his reaction to the room. Tyler had an uncanny way of being able to read someone. Berberidis did not exactly exude a non-judgmental nature. Kirner's leanings were still uncertain. And Javier knew from personal experience that people tended to react strongly with the topic of Dominance and submission were brought up.

If he told them he'd been a practicing Dom, would the police look at him as an aggressor instead of a victim? Would they be able to understand the difference between consensual play and violation? That was why he'd tried to be vague when describing his and Vincent's relationship at first. The stare he was receiving from the detective indicated that Javier really didn't have a choice.

"It's a club that welcomes individuals who support and live a lifestyle of BDSM."

"Jesus H. Roosevelt Christ," Berberidis said under his breath.

Keith walked into the room. "Folks, it's time to clear out. Mr. Alde has an appointment with the orthopedic surgeon to get his knee fixed."

"We're not done yet," Berberidis said.

Keith raised one eyebrow. "You are. For now. Dr. Richards is on rounds and immediate medical care trumps police business. You are welcome to come back later."

Kirner nodded and Berberidis followed him out of the room, mumbling under his breath the whole way. The tension in the room deflated like a balloon the moment the two men were out of sight.

"Thanks," Javier said softly.

"No problem. I saw your blood pressure going up from the nurses' station. Thought a timely intervention was necessary."

Brandon frowned. "So he's not getting a consult on his knee?"

Keith smiled. "Oh, he is." He checked his watch. "In about two hours. Well, I'm going off duty. See you tomorrow, Mr. Alde."

Keith left and Javier looked over at Brandon and Tyler, who wore identical smiles. "I think he just ran a defensive pass interference. I also think it might be time to find a lawyer."

"I already contacted a family friend who's a criminal defense attorney in Dallas. He's on standby," Tyler said.

"Thanks, man, but I really doubt I can afford someone your family knows. Shit, come to think of it, I can't afford anything. No job. No money. No place to live. Fuck, no health insurance. Holy shit, what am I going to do?"

"You're going to let your friend who just happens to come from one of the richest families in the country take care of the financial stuff until you get back on your feet."

Javier shook his head. "No, Tyler. I appreciate it, but I'm not taking your family's money. I know that everything you have is invested in the ranch." Brandon opened his mouth. "And I *know* you don't make enough to pay off hospital fees that are adding up by the second."

"Look, you're used to being Mr. In Charge, but for the foreseeable future, you're going to do what *we* say when it comes to managing anything that involves debt. I will not have you suffering further because of pigheadedness." Brandon stopped ranting and took several deep breaths. "Please?" he asked quietly.

He was clinging to every thread of autonomy he could, because for so long he hadn't been in charge of anything. But in reality, he truly wasn't in a position to turn down Tyler's offer. Which, right now, felt like just one more piercing wound to his soul.

"Yes, Sirs."

"Oh, I could get used to that." Brandon said, rubbing his hands together.

"Shit," Tyler and Javier both said, under their breaths.

Chapter Three

"Well, I already paid a visit to the narco dealer. Are you ready to blow this pop stand?" Brandon asked as he walked into Javier's hospital room.

"More than."

He swung his right leg over the side of the bed with relative ease now that the stab wound had healed — at least on the surface. It would be a while before his muscle strength was completely restored, but he could at least function. One of the reasons he'd been stuck in the joint for so long was because the doctors knew he'd need at least one halfway decent leg to get around on. According to the orthopedist, his knee surgery had been a success, but he wouldn't be able to put weight on his left leg for about three weeks. The full brace helped to stabilize the surgically repaired knee, but he was only a couple of days post-op and a wince escaped as he tried to slide his leg across the bed. "I'm really looking forward to getting an entire night's sleep."

Brandon set the bag of prescriptions on the rolling bed table. "Here, let me help. Um, what should I do?"

Javier smiled. "Hand me the one crutch so I can balance. Keith already helped me get dressed, so at least you don't have to help me get my underwear on. Thank you for bringing the clothes, by the way."

"No problem."

He had trouble catching his breath for a moment as it hit him all over again how Brandon and Tyler had turned their lives upside down to be there for him. When Javier's doctor had said he was being released, he'd had a 'oh fuck' moment as he realized he didn't have anywhere to go and he wasn't exactly firing on all cylinders yet.

"Thank you, again. I'm sorry dealing with me takes you away from Tyler."

Brandon waved him off. "We lived two hours away from each other for the first year and a half we were dating. Time apart is not going to break us. Fortunately, I can work from anywhere. So until the cops get their heads out of their asses and say you can go back to Dallas, it's the Brandon and Javier show."

"Here's your limo, Javier." Keith announced as he brought in a wheelchair.

"Does it have a wet bar?" he asked.

Brandon held up the bag of prescriptions. "Nope. I've got the party mix over here. When can he have another pain killer?"

"I don't want one. I'm tired of being fuzzy-headed."

"Don't be a stubborn ass. You're never going to heal if you're writhing in pain."

Javier stared at Brandon. "I survived months of more pain than you can imagine. This? This is nothing."

A shroud of silence covered the room. Brandon's and Keith's soft breaths seemed to echo. He wouldn't hide from the reality of his abuse, but he refused to let it control him. He was a survivor and, while it might take time, he would get back the life that had been stolen from him.

"I...I don't know what to say," Brandon whispered.

Javier smirked. "Well, that's a first. Look I don't want you walking on eggshells around me, avoiding the giant purple elephant in the room. I have no intention of hiding away or falling into some abyss of depression. I'm not saying it's going to be clear sailing, but if I say I'm good, it's because for the moment I'm good."

"Fair enough." Brandon looked over at Keith. "At least this limo service comes with a hot driver."

Javier chuckled as Keith blushed. He'd miss the guy. Keith had tried to maintain a professional distance, but Javier had beaten him down with kindness until the man had started talking about being a newlywed and they'd struck up a quasi-friendship during Javier's stay. Javier had even given his input on what features Keith and his wife should look for as first-time home buyers.

"Shall we, gentlemen?" Keith asked, gesturing at the wheelchair.

Javier swung his way over and gingerly lowered himself onto the seat. As Keith pushed the chair, Javier said a silent goodbye to each hallway. The lobby of the hospital was the most chaos he'd seen in months. Every muscle in his body tensed and he shifted his eyes from one person to the next. He suddenly had a hard time taking deep breaths. Keith placed his hand on Javier's shoulder and the dizziness faded.

"Brandon, you can bring your car up to the front doors and we'll load up there," Keith said.

Brandon nodded. "Be right back."

Javier turned his head and looked at Keith over his shoulder. "Hey, come around here for a second." As soon as he had Keith in his line of sight, the last of the anxiety dissipated. "I wanted to say thank you. I know you didn't have to come down here to see me off. You're a busy man."

"It was no problem." He leaned in and whispered, "I really was looking for an excuse not to visit Mr. K. He's now taken to cursing us out in Polish."

He found himself laughing, despite his intention to have a serious conversation. "Well, that's fair enough, but no, really. I know I'm probably just room twenty-two fourteen for you and the others, but I really appreciate everything you've done for me and your decency with my friends."

"Hey, none of my patients are just a room number. I make sure to treat everyone on my floor the way I would hope to be treated. Besides, I like your friends. Brandon's kind of a smartass, but he's funny, and Tyler, well, I would never have guessed he grew up a member of America's one percent."

Javier swallowed and nodded. He was a lucky guy to have people like Brandon and Tyler in his life. More than Keith would ever know, considering he'd been a real asshole during his early years.

"I would say I'm going to miss you, but you are a Steelers fan, so…"

"Well, it's not like I can have a guy who's been known to root for the Ravens as a friend anyway."

"Hmm, I guess we're at an impasse."

"I guess so…unless…how do you feel about the Patriots?"

Javier gasped. "Do not speak such blasphemous words in my presence."

"We should be fine, then. Look I don't normally do this, but when you get settled and stuff, give me a call." He held out a piece of paper.

Javier took the scrap and read the digits. It was definitely going over and above, but beside Brandon and Tyler, he really didn't have many other friends in his life. Keith might live in Lubbock and Javier had every intention of going back to Dallas, but nobody ever said they had too many friends.

"Will do. Thanks."

"There's Brandon flagging us down. Let's get you out of here and, no offense, but I really don't want to see you here again."

"None taken."

Keith wheeled him out and when they arrived at the passenger door of Brandon's Jeep, he pushed his way up from the chair and grabbed on to the door frame to stabilize himself, then used the handles to help maneuver into the seat.

"It had to be the left leg, didn't it?" He grunted.

"Don't worry. We're not going too far. I found us a sweet little Airbnb just south of the university. Got a good deal and I figured it was better than sitting on top of each other in a hotel room."

"Thanks. Hopefully we won't have to stay long. I haven't heard anything from the detectives for a couple of days other than 'don't leave town'."

They waved to Keith before Brandon pulled away and Javier dug his nails into the handle above his head. He gripped it harder than was truly necessary.

"So how about some real food? We could grab some takeout or dine-in somewhere, then I'll go get groceries after we get settled. Oh, the place is a guest house on somebody's property. So we'll each have our own room and there's a full kitchen and bath."

"Good. That way I don't have to listen to you and Tyler have phone sex."

Brandon snorted. "Just because there are walls separating us, don't think for one second that Tyler can't make me scream. You have no idea just how good he is."

Javier looked over at Brandon and waited for the lightbulb to turn on.

"Oh, fuck."

Ding!

"Sorry, most of the time I forget at this point that the two of you —"

"Yeah, but you know what you two have is far more meaningful what we did. Not only because you love each other, but your dynamic is completely different. It never would have worked out between Tyler and me, even if I hadn't fucked it up royally."

"Are you talking about the kink stuff?"

"Mmmm, sort of. When I was a practicing Dom, I used the role to purposely create separation between myself and the man I was fucking. I always gave them what they needed physically, but I closed myself off to anything resembling a meaningful relationship. I know that now."

"Not to be nosy, but you keep using the past tense."

Javier nodded. "Just before Vincent — or whatever the fuck his real name was — took me, I'd decided that I needed to reexamine my priorities with my partners. I've known many Dom and subs over the years who find fulfillment in the lifestyle. Some for play, some maintain their roles twenty-four-seven, some just like to fuck and some are looking for committed partners. But I think one of the reasons I never found what I was looking for was because I wasn't doing it for the right reasons."

"So... you're not a Dom anymore? Can you really just turn it off like that?"

"I don't have the answers yet, but I know for damn sure that I'm not looking to get involved with anyone anytime soon."

"Fair enough."

"Besides, it's not as if I don't have enough to deal with at the moment." Javier watched the buildings pass by. "God, I could really go for some jalapeno rings right now."

Brandon tapped on the screen of his phone. "Hey, Siri, find me the best Mexican restaurant near me."

"Okay, here is what I found on the web."

"Pick us a place, man. I'm starving too." Brandon held out the phone

Javier took it and stared at the screen for a second.

"What's wrong?"

"Nothing. It just feels weird to have one of these in my hand again."

"Motherfucker," Brandon whispered.

"No worries. It's like riding a bike, right? I'm sure once I get around to buying one again, it'll be glued to my hands like the rest of our generation."

"We'll go to the store tomorrow and add you to my plan. You're going need one to coordinate your appointments and stuff anyway."

Javier started to object when Brandon turned and gave him the evil eye.

"Thanks," he said, softly.

* * * *

He pulled at the chains that secured him to the ceiling. The metal bit into the already tender and bruised flesh of his

wrists. His shoulders burned from the strain. Sweat poured down his face and stung his eyes.

"You people are all the same. You hide behind the justification of kink, but let's be honest and call you what you truly are. You are a sick fuck who gets off on torturing the innocent."

His voice gone from screaming denials over and over again, Javier just shook his head.

"Stop fucking denying it!"

He screamed as the whip sliced across his back yet again. The trails of fire crisscrossed each other like a map to the hell he found himself in.

"I...I never hurt you."

Vincent punched him in the kidneys, forcing him to swing in his shackles. He knew he'd be pissing blood again. Javier closed his eyes and tried to breathe without throwing up. Vincent didn't like it when he vomited. The bones in his hands ground together as Vincent crushed them in his massive paws.

"Look at me when I'm talking to you!"

He opened his eyes, slowly, and Vincent's face swam inches away from him. The bright blue eyes that had originally attracted Javier glowed and his fair skin was mottled. Rage seemed to drip from every pore of the man's body. When he'd first awoken to this ninth circle of hell, he'd been terrified, even to the point of humiliating himself, but with every slash of the whip and burn of the brand he'd built a casing around his soul. If his body gave up, so be it, but Javier refused to allow this man to destroy his mind.

"What do you want?"

"I want you to admit it. I want you and all of those like you to pay for your perversions. I will eradicate each and every one of you. One by one until our society is cleansed of the stain of your existence."

"First, I'm pretty sure those are some unrealistic expectations. Second, what happens in the privacy of a

person's bedroom is none of your fucking business. Third, if our lifestyle is so abhorrent to you…" He stopped as a cough rattled through his chest. "How come you played the part so perfectly? I think you're just like us. I think this might be one of those 'doth protest too much' situations."

Javier's cheek exploded and the muscles in his neck strained with the force of Vincent's punch.

"Clearly, I have a lot more work ahead of me to make you see the error of your ways. Let's start with a taste of air deprivation."

Javier fell to the floor when Vincent released his chains. Thrashing around, he tried to avoid the hood over his head, but blackness descended with force. Random debris spiked into his flesh as he was dragged across the floor and lifted up onto a hard table. Dizziness swamped him from the steep angle downward. His manacles were secured to the table, as were his feet. Vincent's soft whistle echoed in his ears through the sound of Javier's screams. A weight settled on his face then water cascaded up his nose. He tried to hold his breath, but eventually his body overrode the determination of his brain. He tried to time the phase of the water to suck in a gulp of air. But it wasn't the salvation he hoped. Instead it felt as if a giant wet paw clamped down on his face. Panic invaded as he could no longer tell if he was breathing in or out. Nausea swelled and his ears rang.

"No!" Javier screamed as he jerked up.

Lights flashed and his door was thrown open. Javier threw himself off the side of the bed.

"Oh, fuck!" Brandon shouted.

He curled into a little ball and dragged in as much air as possible.

"Javier, stop. You're okay. You're going to hyperventilate. Take a slow breath in and let it out. That's it. Good. He's gone. He's dead. He can't hurt you anymore."

His brain finally registered that he did have enough air to survive, it was Brandon's voice in his ears not Vincent's, and he was in the bedroom of their rental, not a torture chamber that would have made Torquemada proud.

He'd dead. He's dead. He's dead.

"I killed him," he whispered.

"Yes, you did."

Javier looked up at Brandon. "I'm sorry. Didn't mean to scare you."

"Shut up. Was this the first nightmare you've had?"

He nodded.

"Probably because it's the first time you've had a night where someone hasn't come in to measure you, poke you, change your IV bag and whatever else they did to disturb your sleep."

"I guess it's to be expected. Keith suggested it wouldn't be a bad idea to see some kind of trauma counselor, but I don't really want to sit down with a stranger and relive the last months over and over again."

"You know I'm here for you, but the only thing I know about survivor mentality is from TV and movies. So unless you want my professional skills gained through the University of *The Deer Hunter*, then contacting somebody who actually knows what the hell they're doing might not be a bad idea."

A lightness replaced the inky-dark terror that had pervaded his senses when he awoke. Brandon always found some way to get him out of his head.

"I'll see how things are when we get home. I promise I'll get help if I start getting ideas about the appeal of Russian roulette."

Brandon gripped Javier's shoulder and stared him in the eyes. "You'd better."

"I'm good. I promise."

"Okay. Let's get some sleep. You, uh…you want me to leave a light on or something?"

It probably wouldn't make any difference. Javier figured either he would lie in bed and stare at the ceiling all night or find himself immersed in another horror drawn forth by his subconscious. *But what the hell*

"Sure, thanks."

Brandon helped him back up onto the bed. His knee throbbed, but he didn't think he'd undone the surgeon's repair work by throwing himself onto the floor. The glowing numbers of the clock had indicated that enough time had passed that he could take another pain pill, but he didn't want to risk that the opioid had been the trigger for his dream.

"See you in the morning." Brandon left the room.

"Good night."

Chapter Four

"Thank you for coming in, Mr. Alde."

Javier nodded to Detective Kirner as he made his way on his crutches over to the table. Three weeks after his release from the hospital and he'd finally gotten pretty proficient with the things. He lowered himself into the chair on the opposite side of the table from the detective.

"My client is only too happy to get this ordeal behind him and move on with his life."

Javier almost smirked at the tone of his attorney Wilhelm Logan's voice. The man had been invaluable over the last several weeks, running interference with the police while Javier was in the hospital and in the days immediately after. He'd really been in no place to make any kind of legal decisions that were going to affect the rest of his life.

"Where's Detective Berberidis?" he asked.

"He'll be joining us in a minute, along with the prosecuting attorney. You look like you're moving around better than the last time we spoke."

"I'm getting there. Ribs are just about better and I start physical therapy next week for the knee."

He was really hoping he would be able to do that back in Dallas. Unless, of course, he was going to jail — then he really hoped to be able to get the therapy at all and not end up with a permanent impairment.

"I remember having to do shoulder rehab after a torn rotator cuff a couple of years ago. Some days I would have sworn a baby had more strength than me."

Javier nodded. "My patients always hated the internal rotation exercises the worst after RCT injuries."

"That's right. I keep forgetting that you're a physical therapist."

"Mmhm. Or I was."

"You will be again."

"Will I? Because based on the information my attorney and I have been provided during the course of your investigation, my future is very uncertain."

The door to the interrogation room opened and Berberidis stepped in, along with another man. Both made eye contact with Javier, but neither said anything. Berberidis' face was his usual mask of constipation. The other man carried a file folder. It seemed thinner than Javier would have thought, assuming it had the investigation information.

"Mr. Alde, I'm Peter Masters, the DA of Lubbock County. I'm here to inform you, after reviewing the evidence collected and taking into consideration the circumstances, the State of Texas has decided not to prosecute you for the murder of Luca Pesano, AKA Vincent Finch."

Javier's chest expanded with the first free breath he'd taken since entering the room. It was over. The knowledge that he'd be living with having taken a life had only just taken root in his soul, but at least he didn't have to face being confined to another cell.

"I'm glad to hear you made the right decision, Pete. While my client certainly regrets the death of another man, he clearly had no other option in order to secure his freedom and safety. Mr. Alde will never say the words, but he is, in fact, a hero."

Berberidis grunted, Kirner frowned and Masters appeared to be holding back an eye roll. The door opened and a woman in a black suit entered. Javier had never seen her before, but she carried herself with authority. If he were a paranoid type of person, he'd say she screamed Fed.

"My name is Special Agent Sana Yang with the FBI."

Well, shit.

"Mr. Alde, you've stated that during your captivity, Pesano talked about eradicating the members of the BDSM community one by one. Did he at any time indicate that he'd already been successful in his quest?"

"Why?"

"Just answer the question," Berberidis said.

Wilhelm placed his hand on Javier's arm. "This is a new line of questioning, and I need clarification of your intent. How do Mr. Pesano's possible prior activities affect my client or his newly secured freedom?"

"I have no interest in Mr. Alde's person. The state has chosen not to prosecute and no act he performed defers to the federal level. I am, however, interested in what he knows," Agent Yang stated.

"Is that on record?"

"Yes."

"Can I ask a question?"

"You can ask. I won't guarantee you an answer."

"Well, you're FBI. So that means crimes would have to cross multiple states. I'm from Dallas, so do you know of others like me or are you looking for patterns based on rumors?"

"There are no others like you, Mr. Alde."

"Well, then, not to sound cold-hearted, but why do you care at this point? It's not like you can prosecute him."

Agent Yang opened her folder and set a photo down on the table. Then set down five others that were similar but from different angles. The scar from Javier's brand started to burn all over again. He swore the smell of searing flesh hung in the air.

"I don't need to see the photos. All I have to do is look in the mirror to see what that monster did to me."

Agent Yang slid one of the photos closer to him. "This is you. The others were found on bodies that had been dumped."

"I'm going to be sick." Javier pushed back his chair, Detective Kirner ran over with a trashcan and Javier's stomach quickly evacuated his lunch. When he was able to stop the spasms, every muscle in his body hurt and he felt every single scar that resided on his flesh.

"We know of five other victims. What I'm trying to learn from you is if there are any we don't know about. You're right. We can't prosecute him, but maybe I can find another son or daughter whose family deserves to know what happened to them. Since you're the only person to survive Pesano's attentions, I was hoping you might be able to provide some kind of information that can tell us if this is over or I need to keep searching."

He took a sip of the water that Detective Kirner held out for him. The water in the cup splashed with the tremors in his hand when he moved to set the cup on the table.

"If you knew who he was this whole time, why didn't you stop him? If you knew what he'd done, why wasn't he already behind bars? Why was he able to get to me?" His voice rose till the scream echoed off the concrete walls of the interrogation room.

"Because we failed!" Agent Yang shouted back. "Because I failed. I've been working this case for the past three years. But even using the best profilers in the FBI, we had nothing on the identity of the man who did this. Now that we have a name, I want insight into the way his brain worked. I want to know what wire got jogged lose that triggered his homicidal desires, but specifically made him target persons of alternative lifestyles."

He wanted to know those answers too.

"I'm sorry, but I don't think I can help. It took everything I had just to survive."

"On the contrary. Before your escape all we had were bodies, but no suspects. There was no physical evidence to link an individual to the crimes and none of the victims' family or friends had any idea who they might have been playing with. All we had was a pattern. At least now I can go back to those people and say 'I'm sorry I can't bring back your loved one, but I can tell you nobody else will suffer the way they did.' Not by this man."

"Just try, Javier," Kirner said.

He searched his memory bank. For so much of his time with Vincent—he just couldn't think of him as Luca—he'd been so focused on surviving and maintaining his mental shields that he'd let much of what the man said go in one ear and out of the other.

However, he'd been so desperate to understand Vincent's motives that some things had definitely solidified themselves in his mind.

"He talked about walking through the Presidio and visiting Ellis Island. He mentioned hiking in the Rockies, but I don't know where."

"How come you never mentioned this during our investigation?" Berberidis asked.

"You never asked. Besides, how was I supposed to understand what he was blabbing about was relevant? For all I knew, he was talking about his fucking favorite vacation spots. Besides, I would have told you had you cared about anything more than—"

"Do you believe he targeted you because you're a Dom?" Agent Yang interrupted.

He took a deep breath and let it out. He really disliked Berberidis, and clearly the feeling was mutual. At least after today he wouldn't have to talk to him again.

"No, I don't think he would have cared if I was a Dominant or submissive."

"What makes you say that?"

"Well it was more in his language. It was never 'you Doms need to pay.' It was always 'all you perverts'.

"I'm inclined to agree. Of these five people, three were submissives and two were Dominants, according to their club members."

"So you really don't know anything else?"

Agent Yang shook her head. "Now that we have an identity and an outcome, the Bureau isn't interested in pursuing any other investigation. Federal resources and all. I came here on my own dime. But I'm not ready to let Mr. Pesano go. If I have questions in the future, can I contact you?"

He guessed this was a lesson that reality was not like some movie where the entire plot was wrapped up with a pretty little bow, and the villains laid out their entire manifesto in a monologue with dramatic lighting. It sucked.

"I guess."

"Thank you for your time, Mr. Alde. I wish you the best of luck," Agent Yang said.

"Thank you."

Wilhelm stood, as did Detective Kirner.

"Are we done?" Wilhelm asked.

"Yes. You are officially free to go, Mr. Alde," Kirner responded.

He stood and grabbed his crutches. Berberidis didn't say anything or acknowledge Javier in any way. He followed Yang, Kirner and his attorney out of the room and looked around for Brandon. His friend had been the best over the last several weeks, but Javier knew he was eager to get home to Tyler, even if Brandon wouldn't admit it. Javier found him in a row of chairs, eyes glued to his phone.

"Hey," he said.

Brandon looked up and smiled. "Well, you're not in cuffs."

"Would be a little hard with the whole crutches thing."

"They could get you a wheelchair."

Kirner scoffed. "Please, this is Lubbock. We don't have the budget for actual wheelchairs. We'd probably just stick him in a desk chair, duct tape him to the seat and shove him across the room."

"Sweet! I love a good desk chair race. He's gimpy, so I bet we could take him."

"Wouldn't I get a head start for the disadvantage?"

"No."

Kirner smiled. "Harsh."

Javier shook his head. "You have no idea. So, I can really go home?"

Kirner nodded. "Look, I know Pesano royally fucked up your life, so if you need any help getting back on your feet, let me know. I have a few contacts in Dallas who might be able to help."

"Thanks. We contacted the health and human services people. They have a program to provide short-term emergency financial assistance for disabled indigents to pay for stuff like rent, utilities, transportation and food. I never really thought of myself as disabled or indigent, but I guess I am."

Brandon put his hand on Javier's shoulder. "Only for now. You know you're welcome to stay with Tyler and me."

"I do. But Graham doesn't offer the same options for rehab facilities. Besides, as much as I appreciate everything the two of you have done for me, I need to get control of my life again on my terms."

"Well then, let's hit the road."

* * * *

Despite him being a completely different person, it seemed Dallas and its population had continued their existence without an extra thought. Javier sat outside his former place of work, the Uber driver's words white noise in his ears. He blinked a few times to get the world back into focus. "Thank you. My session will probably last an hour or so. Can I request you to come back and get me?"

"Sure. But there's no guarantees I'll be available."

"I understand." He maneuvered his way out of the car and stared at the glass door. The June sunshine reflecting off the glass blinded him for a moment, but muscle memory was a powerful driver. He pushed the button to automatically open the doors and swung his way inside. It was slightly awkward entering as a patient instead of an employee, but the therapists here were his best chance to get back in fighting form.

"Oh my God, Javier!"

He nearly fell over as he lost his balance on the crutches, because he was startled by the high-pitched exclamation. Clearly Sarah, the therapist who'd taken over his position, hadn't informed the other employees that he was coming in today for his first session.

Thanks so fucking much.

"Hi, Bethany." He smiled as the woman came around the side of the desk and stopped right in front of him. He could see that she wanted to give him a hug, but refrained before taking him in her arms.

"Where have you been? I saw your name on the schedule and I nearly passed out. What happened?"

"It's complicated, but now that I'm ready to get my feet under me again, I knew I could only come to one place for my rehab. I'm just happy that Sarah agreed to take me on as a patient."

"Well of course you had to come here! But, umm, you're not seeing Sarah."

"I'm not? But she said…"

Bethany rung her hands together for a second. "Now that Sarah's the chief, she only sees patients three days a week. And, well, she's not a Medicaid provider."

He sighed. "I understand."

"But hey, you're seeing Malaki Taupo and he's fantastic."

"New guy, I guess?"

"Yes. When Sarah got your job, we hired Malaki to replace her as a full-timer." Bethany leaned in and whispered, "He's really amazing, and total eye candy too."

Javier found himself releasing the tension that had built up. In his fight to survive, he'd forgotten Bethany's ability to make him smile every day. The two of them had always been partners in crime around the office.

"Oh, sweetie, come here."

He didn't even realize tears had formed in his eyes till Bethany swiped them from his cheeks. He found himself wrapped in her arms.

"I'm sorry, Javier, usually we don't make people cry until after the appointment."

He looked up at the deep voice and nearly fell over for a second time in the space of ten minutes.

"Shut up, Malaki." Bethany said while smiling and wiping her own tears away. "Oh, pardon me, how unprofessional."

Malaki made eye contact with Bethany and raised his eyebrow. Bethany's tearful smile turned to a lascivious grin. *Oh yeah, the woman's up to no good.*

Bethany placed her hand on Javier's biceps. "Dr. Alde, this is Dr. Taupo, your therapist."

Javier almost smirked at the way she emphasized their titles. He held out his hand. "Hello. Thank you for seeing me."

Malaki's hands were large and strong. Thick veins snaked up the man's forearms. Javier rarely felt small in life, but at this moment he was dwarfed by the specimen in front of him. His skin gleamed a rich terracotta, much like the brownish-red earth of the Sedona desert.

"We have a lot of work ahead of us. Shall we?"

Javier gripped his crutches, swung past the man away from the reception area and headed for one of the open tables at the back of the room. The place was empty of other patients at the moment. He propped his crutches against the wall and pushed himself up onto the table. He grimaced as he swung his left leg up.

"Here, this might help." Malaki placed a positioning bolster under his knee.

"Thanks. I've been using a pillow at home."

"So, I read the medical chart you had transferred to us. And I saw that your orthopedic care was transferred to Dr. Dorsey at the Lampton Clinic."

"He'd referred patients to me in the past and I called in a favor."

"Well, he's as good as they come, but, as you know, the real work from this point forward is on your shoulders, with me as your guide. Since you know the score, why don't you tell me where you're at?"

"My effusion levels are minimal unless I've really pushed myself. I can walk around my apartment without the crutches, but for long distances I find it easier to have them. I don't have a goniometer at home, but I would estimate that my range of motion is nearly full extension, but maybe only seventy-five percent flexion."

"Okay. What are you doing about pain management?"

"Over the counter NSAIDs, PRN."

"As needed anti-inflammatories are fine as long you're still maintaining your icing schedule, especially after exercise. What about patellar mobilization?"

"I've been doing my thirty reps a day."

Malaki nodded and noted several things on his tablet. "Well, I can see this going one of two ways. Either you're going to be the easiest patient ever or the worst."

Javier knew Malaki was making notes on his case history entries. It was a bit intimidating being on this side of the table. And although Malaki wasn't intentionally trying to make him nervous, Javier still had the urge to peek at what Malaki was saying about him. "Well, we do always say doctors make the worst patients, but I need to get stable enough to find work again soon," he confessed, trying to tease his way out of the awkwardness.

Malaki raised one eyebrow. Javier couldn't seem to stop himself from cataloging each feature of the man's face, from the firm lips to the high cheekbones and over the top of Malaki's shaved head. The man wore the look well, unlike some he'd seen in the past. Malaki was exactly the type of guy Javier would have gravitated toward once upon a time, but there was no way on this green earth he would allow those type of thoughts to take root.

"Don't worry, I'm not after your job. I know I'm going to need to find a new employer."

He didn't know such dark eyes could sparkle or that such a big smile was possible. Malaki somehow transformed from driven therapist to a man whose laugh lines said he experienced pleasure on a daily basis.

"Let's get your brace off and a formal baseline."

* * * *

Malaki sat at his desk, finishing up his chart notes. It was his favorite time of the day, after everyone had left and he had the office to himself. It had been an interesting last few hours. His boss had conveniently taken lunch at the time her former boss had been scheduled for his appointment. Initially, Malaki had been worried that was a sign that Javier was a difficult person, but as it had turned out, that couldn't be further from the truth. The man had a drive to get better, stronger than anyone Malaki had seen in a long time. And given the hug he'd interrupted between him and Bethany, clearly he'd been a well-loved manager.

He looked at the screen. Javier's was the last chart-note he had to complete for the day. The moment Javier's chart had been tasked to his name as the primary provider, he'd locked case-note access to everyone but Sarah. He knew Bethany was desperate to know what had happened to the man, but Malaki protected every patient's privacy to the extreme. If Javier wanted to share, that was his decision. And there really was no way he could prevent Sarah from sharing information with immediate employees, but he sincerely hoped she wouldn't do something like that.

God damn, what he lived through is nothing short of a miracle.

Javier's surgical scar had looked to be healing well, but Malaki had seen other evidence of his ordeal. There was a long scar on his right quadriceps. He'd had an extremely unprofessional desire to touch and soothe away the pain, so much so that he'd clenched his hands into fists, turned his back and spent the most time in his entire career readying the electrotherapy machine.

Just thinking about the scars again got him mad all over. He pushed his chair away and strode out into the exercise area. He needed to move and work some of the tension out of his muscles. He stripped off his shirt with its company logo. The mirrored wall reflected an image that some people considered threatening. He was a large man and his Samoan heritage was enhanced by the massive tattoo that covered the left side of his chest, over the top and back of his shoulder, and down his biceps. He always tried to wear clothing that covered his tattoos at work, but nothing could be done about the fact that muscles covered his body and he towered over most of his patients. He'd specifically sought out a facility that specialized in sport rehab because he didn't want to scare little old ladies trying to recover from broken hips into having a heart attack.

Malaki kicked off his shoes and stripped off his socks. He didn't have any gym shorts on him, so his cargo pants would have to suffice until he got to the gym later. He grabbed the jump rope off the hook and got to work.

After several minutes, his heart rate had sped up to a comfortable pace and Malaki increased his speed. He blinked away the sweat that started to drip down his face. He tightened his core and his slick skin highlighted the ripples of his abdomen. The clutter cleared from his mind, just as he'd hoped. Various small scars from his life as a former collegiate athlete and lifelong enthusiast of extreme sports decorated his body. But they were miniscule and meant nothing to him. Javier's scars were a testament to his strength, and Malaki wanted to make sure he did everything he could to highlight that to the man.

He tossed the rope aside and caught his breath as he walked around the mat. He had so much he needed to do that night. Finish the chart notes and therapy plans for tomorrow, go the gym, stop by the grocery store and complete his meal prep for the rest of the week.

So why do I keep thinking about a pair of soulful brown eyes?

Chapter Five

Sweat ran into his eyes as Javier gritted his way through another set of banded pop squats. His knee burned, and not necessarily in that good 'working his muscles hard' way, but he had to get through this last set. His gaze was locked on the timer Malaki had set up for the cycle of exercises he was supposed to complete. *Is it possible for time to actually slow down?*

"All right, enough," Malaki ordered.

He bent over and tried to catch his breath. It was pathetic how out of shape he was. Before he'd been taken, he could have done a simple circuit like this in his sleep.

"But I didn't...fuck me, that hurts...finish."

"You did three of the four cycles and it won't do you any good if you hurt yourself in the process of rehabbing."

He would have argued some more, but instead he just collapsed onto the mat and tried to hide the fact that tears were starting to mix with the sweat on his face.

Malaki held out a hand. "Come on. Let's get you iced down."

"From your lips to God's ears."

He took Malaki's hand and together they got Javier back on his feet. It was only a dozen or so paces to the table, but Javier's legs wobbled with every step. Finally he reached his destination. Malaki helped him arrange his legs up on the table and slipped the cold water cuff around his knee. Javier laid back and closed his eyes.

"So I know I pushed you today, but you look especially rode hard and put away wet. My keen sense of observation is inclined to think there's something else going on. Want to talk about it?"

He pried his eyes open and tried to focus on Malaki, who leaned against the table next to Javier's.

"What do you mean?"

"We've known each other for a few weeks now. You come in here three days a week. When you first arrived, you were fired up and determined, had this 'nothing's going to take me down' attitude. But lately something has changed. It seems like just getting through your warm-ups does you in."

"I'm doing my best." Javier growled.

Malaki held up his hands. "I know that. I don't doubt your work ethic. In fact, I think you're too hard on yourself. But that doesn't mean I can't see how much you're struggling. Listen, I'm going to step outside my role as a physical therapist for a moment. Are you sleeping? Getting at least six hours a night?"

Six hours would be a dream come true.

"Not exactly," he mumbled.

"Uh-huh. And how about eating? Are you tracking your macros like we talked about? The body can't recover its muscle mass if you're not providing the right type of fuel."

"I could be doing better."

Malaki sighed. "Okay, listen. I'm not going to sit here and lecture you about stuff you know you should be doing. So why don't you talk to me about what's really going on? I've been known to be a pretty good listener and, let's face it, for the next twenty minutes you're not going anywhere."

Javier knew he couldn't keep going on like he was. Lack of sleep was only number one on his laundry list of problems. He jumped at every little sound. If another person snuck up on him, even innocently, he found himself holding back screams. Most nights he ended up haunting his apartment till the pink light of dawn highlighted whatever takeout container he'd left mostly untouched the night before. Of course, none of this meant he wanted to spill his guts to Malaki.

He examined the man waiting quietly beside him. There was no judgment in his eyes or evidence that he was asking out of some sort of determination to pry Javier's deepest secrets from his soul for his entertainment. In fact, Malaki's quiet presence was somehow calming. If he really thought about it, then the only time Javier didn't feel like he was crawling out of his skin was when he was with Malaki.

"I have nightmares."

"About what happened to you?"

He nodded.

"Is it always the same thing? Not that you have to tell me the details."

"No. I mean, sometimes it is, but not always. Sometimes it's about stuff that didn't happen, but I guess my subconscious is convinced might still happen. If that makes any sense."

"Fear is one of the strongest forces in the world. I won't stand here and profess to understand what you went through or try to placate you with empty promises of improvement. But I will say that when I watch you I don't see a man damaged beyond repair. I can only imagine how exhausting it's been to survive and begin your life over again."

Javier nodded. "I'm so tired." He closed his eyes and felt as though the world started to float away. Warmth enveloped his hand and spread throughout his body, chasing away the bone-deep cold that seemed to be his permanent state.

"Then you just sleep for a little while. I'll keep the monsters at bay," Malaki whispered.

* * * *

"How's the therapy going?" Tyler asked.

Javier looked across the small table of the café they'd agreed to meet at, near his temporary apartment. "Which one?"

"Huh?"

"I decided to take Detective Kirner's advice and see a trauma counselor. He put me in touch with one of his contacts here, and I've been seeing him for about two months."

"Well, that's good, I guess."

"Yeah, I think so. I mean, the nightmares were getting worse and I wasn't sleeping. Even Malaki started commenting on how jittery I was and the extra luggage I was carrying under my eyes. He'd noticed how I was losing weight too, instead of building my muscle strength back up."

"Mm, did he now?" Tyler asked, smiling.

"Shut up. It's not like that. He's my physical therapist."

"And I'm sure you have no other interest in the man who you've been working intimately with *and* embodies all your not-so-secret fantasies."

"Fine, so I'm not blind, but it doesn't matter for two very important reasons."

"Please do tell."

It was obvious Tyler was humoring him, by the glint in the man's eyes and the fact that he wasn't even attempting to hide the smile on his lips. Javier was strongly tempted to throw his water in the man's face.

"Fine. First of all, he's a professional and to the same extent I am, too. So, we would never cross a line. Second, I have no desire to start anything with anyone now or even in the future."

Tyler frowned and leaned forward. "Funny that you didn't add to that pathetic list of excuses whether or not you know he's gay. Look, I'm in no position to tell you how to feel or what to think, but I know avoiding relationships altogether is unhealthy."

"I'm not avoiding relationships. I have you and Brandon as friends. I'm social with others in my trauma survivors' group. I just don't want…"

"You don't want to risk your heart again?"

"It was never my heart in danger with him."

"No, it was your life. And you beat him. Don't let that motherfucker steal another second from you. Show his goddamn spirit burning in hell that you're going to live your life to the fullest extent. Love, work and, yes, fuck in defiance of his desires to extinguish you from this earth."

Jesus, he'd never heard Tyler's voice with that hard edge to it before. He understood what Tyler was saying. And his friend wasn't wrong in his thinking, but it just wasn't that easy.

"I can't trust myself," he whispered.

"What do you mean?"

"I never saw it. I never even suspected he was capable of...what he did. I worked with him on an intimate level that went far beyond even that of some long-term partners, but I never saw it."

"Yes, you did. You stopped training him because you knew the dynamic between you wasn't working, right?"

"Yeah, but not that he was a psychopath. Part of the dynamic between Dom and sub is understanding your partner's needs on the most elemental level. He felt the need to, as you said, extinguish me from this earth, and I had no idea. Besides, I don't even think I'm capable of that anymore. Not after everything I went through."

"Capable of what? Tying someone up? Making a man's skin flush and arch into your flogger? Using that deep voice of yours to command a man on the brink of coming to wait until only you allow them?"

He couldn't catch his breath and he stared into Tyler's eyes across the table. An alien feeling of desire made his heart race.

"You forget that I've been there. I've been that man I just described."

"You're not even into the lifestyle. Maybe the fact that I was trying to force it on you should have been my first sign."

"Stop right there. Regardless of how we ended, you know that I was always there eagerly and willingly."

"I hurt you."

"Yes, you did. But not because you were a bad Dom."

"No, I was just a bad person."

"Hey, we're all a work in progress. Besides, I eventually found Brandon and he's completed my life in ways I had no way of understanding I needed at the time we were together. And you? You found what you needed, right? I mean, based on the people I met at that club of yours, you were a hot commodity."

Did I find what I needed? Not really. That was why he'd been reconsidering the whole D/s lifestyle just before being taken. His silence caused Tyler to squint and Javier felt like a specimen being studied.

"I can only imagine how your experience has changed you, so if you no longer want or need that kind of relationship with someone, it's your choice. Maybe start with a cup of coffee instead of a session at the Citadel. Speaking of which, have you at least been back to see the people there since returning to Dallas?"

He shook his head. "I've started to several times, but I always chicken out before I can open the door."

"Okay. So maybe invite your closest friends from there to a neutral location? When Brandon and I were searching for you, I could see how worried they were. Those people care about you."

"I know. I know. I'll call Everett and Henry."

"Good. Now, the reason I actually asked you to meet me today is because I had some good news to share. Wilhelm, a forensic accountant he recommended and I have been looking into what happened to all your money since your kidnapping. That fucker was smart and evil, but my people are smarter."

"What?"

"The forensic guy was able to trace the money from the moment it left your bank. I gave him your former account numbers, by the way. The money went through a series of electronic transfers into several dummy holdings, but it eventually landed in the Cayman Islands."

"What?"

"You keep saying that. So anyway, I contacted the bank as the head of the newly formed Synder Foundation for Asset Restitution and provided them with the documentation, obtained by Wilhelm, and a court order necessary to release the funds."

"The Synder who?"

"Okay, so I'm not above using my family name to open a few doors. At first, they said no, since a US court order has no real power in a British overseas territory, but it helped that this particular bank knows my family because we've also got assets invested with them. I might have casually mentioned that we would withdraw our funds and take them someplace else if they didn't comply."

"Wait, would you really have done that?"

Tyler grinned. "Well, no. It's not *my* money so much as the family's and part of the corporation's. But they didn't know that or didn't look that far into it, anyway. So long story short—"

"Too late."

Tyler slid a piece of paper across the table. "Here is the register information and balance. You can contact them to transfer the funds into the account you opened when you got home."

"Wait a minute. Even if the money was stolen from me, the account was in Luca's name. So wouldn't his assets get distributed to his next of kin or whatever?"

"We contacted Agent Yang and she unofficially told us that Luca doesn't have any surviving relatives that are in a position to make a claim and the bank does not have a beneficiary on file for the balance in the event of his death."

Javier's hand shook as he slid the paper across the table. He couldn't believe Tyler had gathered a crew and they'd gone to so much effort. Wilhelm, the attorney, had already gone to bat for Javier with the Feds, so it no longer seemed that he'd defaulted on his student loans from graduate school. Fortunately, they were now in deferment until he got another job, but every day more interest was building up. It wasn't as if Javier had been rolling in cash before his disappearance, but he'd had an income and small savings account. Right now, he was living off his disability income with the additional benevolence of the Synders. And as much as he acknowledged that he wouldn't have been able to survive the last couple of months without their help, it also significantly bit into his ego. To have something, even one little thing, from his old life back felt monumental. He opened the paper and gasped.

"Tyler, what the fuck? I didn't have this kind of money!"

"Yeah, I suspected that might be the case. Otherwise PTs make a whole lot more money than I thought. Wilhelm and our helpful friend suspected that this account was a holding pen for all the victims' assets, plus his own investments. The problem is we have no way of determining what money belonged to whom.

We were not privy to the details of the FBI's investigation. So maybe they could match up deposit dates with timelines of the other victims, but from my perspective, the ball is really in your court what to do with it."

He couldn't take all of it. There was no way. Just because the others had died didn't mean that he should be awarded for surviving.

"Maybe I can contact Agent Yang and ask her what the right thing to do is? The last thing I want is some family member finding out then coming after me for liability. You think she'd tell me the names of the others or maybe she can contact their families and we can work something out?"

"I think that would be very gracious of you. I would suggest you don't get directly involved with any money transfers. Contact Wilhelm and ask him about setting up some kind of trust or something. Now I hate to cut this visit short, but I have a mare that could drop at any moment, a partner who if left alone for too long will forget to feed himself, and a two-and-a-half-hour drive ahead of me."

Javier stood and wrapped his arms around Tyler. "Thank you."

Tyler gave Javier a strong pat on the back. "You're welcome. And since I didn't say it earlier, it's good to see you on your own two feet."

"Yeah, Malaki is amazing. Might even give me a run for my money as the best physical therapist in town."

"Uh-huh. But you don't feel anything other than professional respect towards the man. Oh, and about the other therapist, I'm glad you're getting help. Malaki wasn't the only one who noticed the changes, you know. We just didn't really know how to talk about it, without talking about it. You know?"

"I know. You can promise Brandon that he doesn't need keep checking on me every day."

"Yeah, like he ever listens to me."

"Oh, I'm pretty sure he listens sometimes. I'm not the only one with a voice that can get people to come at my command."

Tyler winked as he walked away.

Javier blew out a breath. He had Agent Yang's contact info back at his apartment, but there was one number he knew by heart. He'd talked a big game about taking back his life, but in reality he'd been scared of how people would treat him after finding out what had happened to him. There was only one way to find out.

He took out his phone and dialed. The ringing gave him just enough time to reconsider his resolve.

"Hello?"

"Ev…Everett? Hey, I…um, how are you?"

"Holy fuck, Javier? Where are you?"

"I'm at the Coffee House Café in North Dallas."

"Do not move. Henry and I are on our way."

It was Monday and the club was closed. Normally Everett and Henry reserved the day for themselves, and while he was under no obligations to follow Everett's command, he found himself sitting in his chair and ordering another iced coffee.

It only took about twenty minutes before Everett's car pulled up right outside the café's patio. He stood as his friends exited the vehicle. At first glance, both Everett and Henry looked the same, but there were subtle differences. Tiny worry lines ran across Everett's forehead and Henry's bright complexion didn't have its usual rosy undertones.

"Sir, I can't believe it's you. Where have you been? We've been looking for you," Henry blurted.

Javier took a hasty step back as Henry practically bounced his way over from the car with his arms outstretched. Henry's face fell and Javier felt about two inches tall. He'd never shied away from the man's habitual enthusiastic greetings before, but for some reason he panicked at the thought of being wrapped in Henry's long arms.

He smiled. "Hey. Umm, sorry. I didn't mean anything. It's really great to see you guys."

Everett took Henry's hand and he immediately gravitated towards his partner. Everett didn't try to approach him, and he actually felt disappointed.

You're a giant fucking mess.

Three of them sat down and silence enveloped the table. Javier cleared his throat, unsure how to start the explanation that Everett and Henry deserved.

"Okay, enough stalling. You're going to tell us where in the hell you've been."

"It's a rather—"

"Do you know that we searched every hovel and high-end hideout for weeks? You told Henry you'd be coming back, and yet your car haunted my parking lot until it mysteriously disappeared three weeks later. It was then that I figured it was safe to assume that the man I thought was my friend was really an unprecedented twat."

"You looked for me too?"

"Of course we looked, you arsemonger! In fact, despite all evidence pointing to the fact that you'd simply became a ghost, I still called every owner of a public club in the US asking if you'd registered as a member. Some of them even gave me tips on private invite only organizations in their area. But after calling in every favor I was owed there was still no sign of you. It was like you disappeared into a black hole."

"That's not actually far from the truth. Except the black hole was actually a concrete cell."

"You went to prison? For what? And if that was the case, why did some tall cowboy come looking for you?" Henry asked.

"Not prison, no. I...I was taken." He inhaled and let out the breath slowly then recounted his experiences since last October. As he spoke, Everett's expression turned harder and Henry's went from simply pale to a grayish green. Their hands locked together and while he didn't tell them everything, he told them enough, and quite frankly more than he'd shared with Tyler and Brandon.

"I'll fucking kill him," Everett growled.

He looked his friends in the eyes. This was a moment of truth.

"I did."

The only thing Javier heard was the clinking of the utensils from other diners on the patio and the whoosh of an occasional car passing by. He found himself holding his breath, waiting for the verdict.

Is this what it would have felt like if the DA prosecuted me for murder?

Had life gone another way, would he be sitting behind a table waiting to hear the decision from a jury instead of at a café sipping an iced latte? He had a feeling the clammy sweat dripping under his collar would be the same.

"I'm glad, Sir."

Javier studied Henry's eyes. There was never an emotion the man had been able to hide in the most guileless pair of green eyes Javier had ever seen. There was no fear or disgust evident in Henry's gaze. He glanced over at Everett, who was harder to read. Everett had been in the right to read him the riot act based on their knowledge, but now that the entire narrative had changed, how would his and Everett's friendship evolve? Would there still even be a friendship? Everett's expression didn't give anything away, but his body language remained open, something Javier took as a good sign. Everett gave the slightest of nods and a rush of relief swept through him so fast he got a little dizzy.

"Henry, I know your training has you using that term as a way of respect towards me as a Dom." Henry nodded. Javier didn't want to hurt the sub's feelings or confuse him. "I don't know if my future lies with the BDSM community any longer, or at least in the same way as I was. Will you do me the honor of addressing me as Javier, from this point forward?"

Henry looked to Everett and the silent communication between the two of them conveyed more than a dictionary full of words. Everett nodded and Henry's eyes held that familiar glow of happiness once again.

"I'll do my best to remember."

"Thank you. Now tell me all about what the two of you have been up to and all the good gossip."

"Oh my, we're going to need something more than iced coffee." Henry cheered.

* * * *

Javier pulled open the door to the rehab facility. It was a big day. The dog days of August were upon them, and he was officially ten weeks post-op. Malaki had scheduled his first sports assessment for today. Javier might not be a full-time athlete anymore, but his primary goal was to get back into the kind of shape he'd been before his ordeal. He needed to have the endurance and strength to work with clients again.

"Hey, Bethany, what kind of tortures does he have for me today?"

"Only the best kind. I promise." She winked.

Out of the corner of his eye, Javier saw Malaki raise one eyebrow. Javier's question had been entirely innocent, but once the innuendo came out he did his level best not to look directly at Malaki. He didn't want the man to think he and Bethany had been gossiping about him in an inappropriate way.

"If I've done my job right, then you'll be gasping for breath and have sweat dripping from your body. Your heart will be racing, and you'll look at me with a perfect blend of hate and appreciation."

And cue the mental porno.

It wasn't until he and Malaki were halfway across the floor that the realization hit that he'd just been joking about being tortured. He looked down at his left forearm, where the raised lines of one of the branding scars testified to his knowledge of real torture.

"Hey? You okay?"

He found his feet cemented to the floor. Malaki glanced around the room then came over and stood so close that Javier was forced to look up at him. His dark eyes held remorse, but Javier liked it much better when they were bright with happiness.

"I'm sorry. I didn't think." He looked down at Javier's arm. "The patches seem to be helping with the scar tissue."

Malaki's soft voice floated over the top of his head and Javier caught his breath. A shiver raced through his body and he became lightheaded for a moment.

Holy shit no, we are not going there!

"You didn't do anything wrong. And thank you for the tip about the patches. I'm not sure how much of the improvement is from them or just natural healing, but they seem to be better. And you know I stopped cold, because it hit me that I didn't think either. Kind of cool, right?"

Malaki started to reach for Javier, but stopped before they touched. "Yeah." Malaki cleared his throat and stepped back. "So, ready to get to work?"

"I'm under your command."

Shit. Stop perving on your therapist.

Malaki mumbled something as he walked toward the stationary bike, but Javier didn't catch it.

"So, let's do your usual ten-minute warm-up on the bike. Then I've got everything set up for your test."

"Sounds good." Javier climbed up on the bike and set the program. "So, how's everything going here?"

Malaki looked around. "I never talk about business stuff with a client."

Right. These aren't my coworkers and friends anymore. I'm just another chart number.

"But it's different with you."

Oops. Pity party table of one, please.

"Sarah quit."

"What!" Javier lost his footing on the bike and winced at the slight torque to his knee.

"Yeah. She just came in the other day and said she'd been recruited by a subcontractor for the VA doing compensation and pension exams. She basically said that she was getting more money for only working three days a week."

Javier whistled softly. He'd been the one to hire Sarah only a few months before he'd been taken. "That sucks."

"Yeah. I mean, I get it she has to do what's right for her family. She does have two kids, and I know it's been tough on her trying to balance being a manager and a parent. But I can't help but feel like we're getting dumped."

"When's her last day?" He should at least wish her luck.

"Two weeks from now."

"Jesus, nothing like giving the company enough time to find a replacement."

Malaki smiled. "Yeah. So, want your old job back?"

Javier whipped his head around so fast he almost feared he'd be coming to see Malaki for a whiplash injury next. The idea of working again doing what he loved was the biggest carrot Malaki had been dangling in front of him for weeks. But he knew he wasn't ready.

"Umm…how about you?"

"Me?"

"Sure, why not? You're a great therapist." Javier held out his arms and kept peddling. "Obviously. It seems like everybody around here respects you. I know you're smart enough. I mean, Bethany's always saying under her breath, 'WWMD'."

"WWMD?"

"Yeah. What would Malaki do?"

His heart fluttered a little at Malaki's deep laugh.

"Well, in all likelihood, Vista will send a manager from another location."

Javier shrugged. "Maybe, but I still think you should submit. I mean, you've been a PT for how long now?"

"Well, let's see…what year is it?"

"I think it's 2017. Unless I've managed to lose several months of time again."

"Not to worry. I've been keeping a careful eye on you."

Have you, now?

"Okay. Let's do the math. I spent eight years in San Diego, then three years in Washington and the last four years I've had a bit of wanderlust as a traveling PT."

"Wow. Are you still under contract with the traveling agency? Because that would make a difference."

"No. My last job was here in Dallas and I found that I liked the city. So when this full-time position was posted, I applied and was thrilled to get it."

Javier did the math and realized that Malaki was older than he'd thought.

"I still think you should submit your name for consideration."

"Tell you what, I'll think about it. Now, let's get you over to the Airex pad. Your first task is a stability test."

Javier climbed off the bike and rubbed his hands together. "Bring it on."

Chapter Six

Javier sat in front of his laptop with a beer, staring at the screen. His résumé stared back at him in black and white. He'd passed his test with flying colors. His talk with Malaki and his most recent session with his therapist had really made him realize that he was ready to get back to work. He didn't want the stress of a management position again, not yet, but craved the challenge of getting a person back to their daily routine.

In the two months since Javier had contacted the bank in the Caymans, the money had made a big difference in him regaining his independence, but it didn't feel right relying on ill-gotten gains. His knee was strong enough for light-to-moderate activity. And he had his functional brace, if more strenuous activity was required. After spending an afternoon searching for jobs online, he'd narrowed down the options to his top choices. Now, it was just a matter of sending out his résumé and hoping one of the facilities responded with interest. His phone vibrated beside him, and he looked down but didn't recognize the number.

"Hello?"

"Hey, what are doing?"

"Malaki? How did you get my number?" *Right – he's got all my information at his fingertips.* "Never mind. Stupid question. I'm sitting here trying to find opportunities to be a productive citizen again. You?"

"I'm sitting here looking at apartments and thought local might help me narrow down a good area that won't destroy my budget."

"You want to move?"

"The place I've been staying only had a short-term lease. When I was doing the traveling gig, it was perfect, but since I've decided to stay, I'm going to need some permanent digs."

"Gotcha. I'm actually in the same boat, but I'll need to find a job first to figure out my budget."

"Where are you staying now?"

"It's…um…well it's a housing authority property in North Dallas. Brandon and Tyler made the arrangement when I was still in Lubbock. It's worked out fine and I am very grateful, but I think it's time to stand on my own two feet. No pun intended."

"Those are your friends with the ranch, right?"

"Yeah. Well, it's Tyler's ranch." Javier chuckled. "Brandon likes cowboys, but he's not exactly one himself. He's a graphic artist. Does book covers."

"You've talked about them a lot. Must be good friends."

"They are. I've had a lot of casual friends over the years, but they're different." He scoffed. "From the outside, our friendship probably looks pretty fucked up, but we're solid."

"What do you mean?"

"Have you ever made a choice that seemed unquestionable, but ended up being harmful in ways you really couldn't understand at the time?"

"I think regrets on some level are a part of everyone's life."

"Yeah, well, I made some choices in my younger years that to some made me seem irredeemable. In my struggle to accept myself I treated Brandon and later Tyler in ways that make me ashamed. It wasn't until the three of us were faced with each other again that I found the strength to ask for their forgiveness. We'd probably be a great case study for some psychology Ph.D. candidate."

"Sometimes it's the people we share the most troubled past with that become the most meaningful in our lives."

That sentence was true on more than one level. It was why Javier continued to wake up screaming in the middle of the night and he had a small bottle of pills that sat in his bathroom cabinet. But it was also why he'd felt safe enough to let Brandon hold him when he'd been watching some stupid show on TV and the tears just wouldn't fucking stop.

"Javier?"

He cleared his throat. "Yeah. Yeah, I'm here. Sorry. So, apartment shopping, huh? Well, I can give you a few pointers, I guess."

"Great. Why don't we meet for a beer and I'll bring some of the listings I was looking at?"

"Sounds good. Um, not to be anal or anything, but is this cool with me still being your patient? Not that I don't want to hang out or think it bad — in fact, it's weird that I don't think it's wrong, because I never gave out personal info or socialized with my patients before. Oh, fuck it, I'm just going to shut up now."

"No, no, I get you. In fact I was going to throw out the question if you had any desire to come back to the good old Southwest?"

He thought about it for about half a second.

"I don't. It has nothing to do with the place or even the people. I love Bethany and, believe it or not, I think we'd make good colleagues. But I think I need a fresh start."

"That's a shame, because I was hoping my first act as chief PT would be hiring you."

"You got it! I totally knew you would."

"Thanks for talking me into submitting. I realized after you left that day that I'd gotten comfortable in my routine. It wasn't until I really did the math with you that I became aware of just how long I'd been doing the same thing day after day. If I want my career to move forward I need to take the next step and that's having management experience."

"Not that I had any doubt, but that was really a quick turnaround for corporate."

"It was kind of funny. When I contacted them, they basically said yes before I even got off the phone with them. I received the official offer and letter of hire the next day."

"I think your first order of business will be to clean out that office. I know that when it was mine, there were journal articles with curled and discolored page and paperwork that was so obsolete it should have been shredded years ago. I'd been slowly working my way through the piles, but had barely made a dent. Knowing how much of a packrat Sarah was, she didn't advance the effort."

"Ugh, yeah, not looking forward to that part."

"Don't worry. I'll help. Oh, I mean, that is, if you want me to?"

"Of course I do! In fact, the whole hanging-out thing won't be an issue, because I'm going have to transfer some of my caseload to another provider. I was thinking McKayla would be a good fit for you."

Javier found himself letting out a big breath. "I like her no-bullshit attitude. She'll keep me on my toes and keep pushing me."

"Great. Then maybe we can make a night of cleaning the office after one of your therapy sessions. I'll even buy dinner."

"Real working dinner or one of those poached protein-laden-health-conscious fuel sources you're always talking about?"

"You've gotten lazy. You need more of those healthy fuel sources if you're going to get back to where you were before. We've talked about your meal plan. Are you following it?"

"Yes, Mom."

"Dude. There is so much wrong with that I don't know where to start. Listen, I have to go, but I'm serious about getting your input on where to hang my hat."

"Hang your hat? What are you, like, eighty?"

"I'll show you just what this old man can do."

Javier looked down as his cock jumped.

Just what the hell do you think you're doing?

"Oh, it is on like Donkey Kong. I'll bring my résumé and you can give me some input. It's been a while since I updated it and I'm going to need every edge I can to get a job again. I'll see you tomorrow night. Seven sharp. Los Sapitos on East Jefferson."

"Hasta luego, mi amigo."
"Buenas noches."

* * * *

Malaki spun the cardboard coaster around and sipped his beer as he waited for Javier to show up. The excuse about getting the man's input on finding an apartment was seriously lame. He was surprised that Javier hadn't seen right through it. It wasn't as though he'd reached the age of nearly forty without the ability to find a place to live.

Ever since they'd reduced Javier's therapy sessions to once per week, he'd found himself searching out any reason to talk to the man. Now that McKayla was taking over as his therapist, he'd have even less time with him. All throughout the day they'd been flinging texts at each other, some even with those stupid bitmojis. He was reasonably sure that Javier liked him as a friend, but what was still very murky was if the man had any feelings beyond the platonic. There were times when Malaki saw something deeper than friendship in Javier's eyes, but then he'd make some kind of pithy comment and deflect harder than the heat shields on the International Space Station.

Javier hadn't really talked in detail about what had happened to him or the circumstances leading up to his being taken, but Malaki had deduced enough to know that the man responsible was someone Javier had dated. It wasn't illogical to think that would make the man a bit gun shy.

"Plotting world domination?"

He looked up and swallowed his sip of beer very slowly. Javier stood tall in front of him, dressed in a royal blue T-shirt that set off his dusky complexion perfectly. His bare arms revealed that the man was finally starting to build up muscle tone again. Malaki had seen old photos of Javier, and while he certainly knew what malnutrition and dehydration did to the body in a physical sense, witnessing their effects on Javier had been difficult. That didn't even include the further deterioration on his body from the trauma and stress of the infection he'd been treated for in the hospital.

"What?"

"You looked really deep in thought. I just figured you were either plotting world domination or single-handedly solving the mysteries of the universe."

"Actually, I was trying to decide if I wanted chicken wings or spinach artichoke dip for an appetizer."

Javier sat and picked up a menu. "Hmm. Yes, that is a tough choice, although the only correct answer is bell pepper nachos."

He couldn't resist smiling into those dark brown eyes for a moment. "Sold."

"Sweet. Brandon never lets me get away with the ultra-spicy stuff. So, anything good happen today?" Javier asked, sitting down.

"Good for me in that I have a new challenge. Started therapy with a seventeen-year-old. Spinal cord concussion."

"Damn. I've always been incredibly grateful that I survived my playing years without any major injuries."

"You were a running back?"

Javier shook his head. "Wide receiver. All-American, thank you very much."

"How come you didn't go for the draft?"

"Well, there's a long answer and a short answer to that question. The short answer is I didn't want to play pro-ball. The long answer is much more complicated…" Javier looked around the room. "And probably better discussed not in public."

Malaki raised an eyebrow.

"How do you do that?" Javier asked, laughing.

"I don't know. I just do. It's kind of like that smoldering look you have. Unless you're more calculating than I ever gave you credit for."

"I have a smoldering look?"

"Oh yeah."

"What's it look like?"

Malaki closed his eyes and did his best to show Javier. But instead Javier started cracking up.

"Shut up!" He flung the coaster at Javier.

"I'm sorry, but if that is supposed to be my sexy look, it's shocking I ever got laid at all."

"Fucker. I didn't say I could do it." He unlocked his phone. "Now try being useful and show me where to live."

Javier scooted his chair over to Malaki's side of the table and he might or might not have inhaled the man's scent just a bit longer than necessary. They flipped through Malaki's top choices and weeded out the ones that had good marketing, but were poor in reality. Their appetizer was delivered, and the little moans that came out of Javier's mouth had Malaki tightening every muscle in his body in effort to stop him from reaching out to touch the man.

It was the worst and best dinner that Malaki could remember. He clearly had some masochistic tendencies he'd never realized, because only a fool would seek out the torture of spending so much time in close proximity with a man who was so far off-limits.

"Can I ask you a question?" Javier whispered.

Malaki nodded.

"Did you really need my help?"

He shook his head.

"So this was all an excuse to see me outside the office?"

He nodded again

"Why?"

Panic flared in Javier's eyes and Malaki cursed softly. This wasn't the time or the place. And he'd actually been really selfish in asking Javier to play a game when the other man didn't know the rules.

"At some point, I promise I'll tell you. Until then just know that I enjoy a good beer and pleasant company from time to time."

Javier let out a long breath and his shoulders relaxed as if a great weight had been lifted. Malaki's gut twisted with disappointment, but he knew he'd made the right decision.

He believed to the marrow of his bones that Javier was meant to hold an intrinsic place in his life. Whether that was purely on a level of friendship or something more intimate, only time would tell. It was a good thing Malaki was a patient man.

* * * *

"So this is where all the magic happens," Malaki said as he showed Javier the bedroom of his new condo.

"Does your magic involve others suddenly disappearing, because it's kind of sparse in here?"

"I've never had complaints before."

I'll bet. Just look at him. Stop! No, no looking, because you know damn well that you're not going to touch. But you want to touch. In fact, you want to touch very much. Great, now I have rhyming voices in my internal monologue.

"That's it! That's that smoldering look."

"What?"

Malaki cleared his throat. "Never mind. So, yeah, I know it looks pretty pathetic right now, but I still have to buy all the stuff to put in it. I've only been renting furnished places for the last few years, so I have nothing of my own."

"Seriously?"

"Just my clothes and a few knick-knacks. When I first started the traveling gig, I had stuff from my apartment in San Diego, but quickly learned it was a pain to move it all every few months. So I sold everything but my truck."

"Wow. So you went from a total transient to a home owner. That's like a big one-eighty. Are you having any symptoms of vertigo? If so, I would recommend a great PT for rehabilitation. Except he's currently unemployed."

"That last interview didn't work out, huh?"

Javier shook his head. "But honestly I only submitted my résumé there because I'm getting desperate. It's been a month. I've had four interviews and four rejections. When I graduated, I literally had my pick of employers. If my ego were more fragile, I'd start to think I smelled bad or something."

Malaki's deep laugh filled the room and Javier found himself a few steps closer to the man before he realized it was happening.

"Trust me, you don't smell bad. In fact, even dog-ass tired, sweaty and reduced to grunts, you look and smell delectable."

Javier swallowed. All the hairs stood up on his body like tiny antennas, seeking out the signal from the heat in Malaki's gaze. "Was that your word for the day?"

"Nope, it was actually feisty."

"Can you use that in a sentence?"

"How about, 'I love a feisty man between the sheets'?"

Oh, dear God, we have reached Defcon level two.

Javier wanted Malaki. He was able to accept that.

The problem lies in the fact that I wanted Vincent too, and Tyler and every other man I hooked up with over the years.

Feeding that want was what had led him to hurting the man who'd become an important friend, then to a series of unsatisfying relationships.

And ultimately to the horror that still has me haunting my apartment at night to avoid succumbing to the terrors of my subconscious.

"Right, so all new furniture huh? That's either going to be a lot of fun shopping for or a total nightmare. Did you really think that out all the way?"

"I've been saving to buy for years, just didn't know where I'd land. Besides, this way I've had time to think about what I really want."

"Well, I have to say this is a nice place. I know it was a hassle waiting the extra month to close with all drama of the previous owners, but totally worth it to score the unit you wanted. The whole modernist feel with a homey touch is very you."

"Oh no, too much HGTV has rotted your brain. We need to get you a job fast."

"You might be right. There are times that I feel that if I hear the words shiplap or open concept one more time, I'll scream."

"There's a great solution to your problem."

"What's that?"

Malaki stepped closer and leaned down to whisper in Javier's ear, "Change the channel." He started walking towards the bedroom door. "Or you can come over here where I only allow movies with gratuitous violence and big explosions. Preferably with ultra-hot alpha studs in shredded clothing."

Javier's fingers twitched with the desire to grab Malaki's hips and push him against the nearest wall. However, it was just that kind of urge that had gotten him into trouble in the first place. Hell, it had been weeks since their dinner out and other than the occasional comment like earlier, or innuendo, Malaki hadn't said anything more about something between them. Much to his relief. Because Javier didn't know what the hell he wanted anymore.

He hadn't felt this insecure about life since he was in high school and denying his sexuality. It was as though his brain had completely short-circuited when it came to sex. To add insult to injury, he hadn't even managed to get hard, other than his typical morning wood. Every time he tried to jack off, his dick refused to come to attention, and his fantasies were a black hole of nothingness.

"Hey, you okay?"

Javier blinked several times and realized that Malaki was standing in the doorway, watching him.

"Yeah, sorry, was just thinking of stuff." A few steps and he paused right in front of Malaki, filling the door frame, arms stretched over his head. "Move, you behemoth."

"Make me, you scarecrow."

Javier growled and gripped Malaki's forearms. Jesus, his fingers didn't even encircle the cords of muscle or make a dent in the flesh. He pushed, but Malaki didn't move. A low chuckle fueled his ire, and he slid his hands up to Malaki's wrists to get better leverage. It wasn't until their chests pressed together that he realized they'd never been closer. There was an odd tingle in his gut, and he lost his balance as Malaki stepped back quickly. A flare of pain went through his knee and Javier winced.

"Shit, I'm sorry." Malaki reached out to steady him.

He held up his hands and stepped away. "I'm fine. Didn't realize I was leaning into you. Sorry."

"No, it's my fault. I was just messing around, but should have known better. What do you say we get out of here? I have some furniture shopping to do, and you said you've got a meeting?"

Javier looked at his watch. "Shit, yeah."

"Another job interview?"

"No, FBI."

"Everything okay?"

Javier brushed past Malaki now that the man wasn't impersonating a brick wall. "Oh yeah, fine. It's just about the case. Some final details and stuff. You should check out Langham's. They're a consignment shop for upscale stuff. Probably won't find chairs and stuff to fit you, but lots of other good stuff."

"Thanks. Are you sure you're okay? You had a...I don't know...worried look on your face before."

"I'll figure it out. I'm still just trying to find normal again, you know?"

"That's fair. I know you've got Tyler and Brandon, but you know I'm here if you need me."

He nodded. The problem was that most of his conflict had to do with these urges and feelings about the very man offering to help. Talk about awkward.

"Good."

As they walked out of the door, there was a man standing by the swimming pool. His trunks rode low on his lean hips as he stretched his arms high above his head and swung his arms to loosen up. Malaki sucked in a gasp.

"I guess the new house comes with a view," Javier said.

Malaki mumbled something. Javier didn't catch it. He waved when the man looked up at them and did a double take at the sight of Malaki. He did not like the slow eye-fuck coming from the man as Malaki walked toward him. Javier hung back as Malaki introduced himself and the two chatted for a minute. The guy glanced his way then back at Malaki. Javier's gaze collided with a pair of narrowed dark brown eyes and a frowning mouth. It was at that moment he realized he was grinding his teeth and clenching his fists.

What the hell? Okay, item twenty-two to discuss in therapy this week.

He shook out his hands and signaled to Malaki that he was headed towards the car. As he passed through the gates to the front parking area, the sound of running steps came from behind him.

"Wait up!"

Javier turned, but kept walking backwards. Maybe he could just play it off as though he hadn't unintentionally cock-blocked his friend. "Hey, I gotta run, but I'll see you tomorrow."

He ran to his car before Malaki could say a word.

Chapter Seven

"Thank you for agreeing to help me, Agent Yang."

"This is an unusual request, but given the circumstances, I'm inclined to help. You do realize that the families may be unwilling to talk to you?"

"I do, and I'll respect their wishes. It just seems wrong not to try."

"That's admirable. We'll try the Carsons first. I'll initiate the call and introduce you, then let you take over."

"Okay. They're the parents of the man from San Francisco, right?"

Agent Yang nodded as she dialed on the desktop phone and the ring pierced the room. He winced at the volume. Nerves were making him jumpy. All last night and this morning before he'd met Malaki, he'd thought about what he wanted to say. They didn't exactly make a Hallmark card for this situation.

"Hello?"

"This is Agent Yang with the FBI. Is this Mr. Carson?"

"Yes, I didn't expect to hear from you again. Is there some new information about my son's killer?"

"In a way. I'm here with a man named Javier. He was another victim of Mr. Pesano's, and has some information he wanted to share."

"I thought all the other victims died?"

Agent Yang looked at him and Javier saw the silent question in her eyes.

"I nearly did, sir. I was held captive and tortured for seven months."

"How did you escape? I thought the police didn't have any suspects, or was it just pure luck that they found you?"

Maybe he was listening too hard, but he thought there was a hint of resentment in Mr. Carson's voice. He could understand the sentiment, since the man had been forced to bury his son and Javier was alive and mostly well. He looked at Agent Yang. He wasn't sure if he could divulge any information with legal implications. She nodded and the ball was in his court. He'd been working really hard with his therapist in coming to terms with not only his time in captivity, but also how it had come to an end.

How it came to an end? You need to say the words. Stop letting them have power over your life.

"Hello?"

"I...I...I killed him."

He heard a loud expulsion of breath over the phone, then silence. Javier looked at Agent Yang.

"Hello?" she asked.

"I know there's an appropriate response to your announcement, but the only thing running through my head is 'thank fucking God'. Is that what you wanted to tell me?"

"No, sir. It…um, it came to light afterwards that there was a bank account that held the confiscated assets of all the victims. With the help of a forensic accountant, I was able to claim the contents as the only survivor. There's no way to separate the exact holdings by individual, and I don't feel comfortable keeping everything. I know that money will never bring back your son, but some of the assets rightly belonged to him and therefore you."

"There're many things I learned about my son and his life during the investigation. Some of them I really don't understand or quite frankly didn't need to know. However, there is one absolute that will never change. I love my son, and whatever you found in that account will never mean as much to me as he did. Keep the money to restart your life or give it away. I don't care."

"I'm sorry, sir. I wish I had something else to offer you."

"You can make the best of your life. I don't know how you came into contact with that monster, but all I ask is that you take precautions. Don't…don't put yourself into a dangerous situation that risks this second chance you have at life."

"That's a promise I can make, sir."

He felt as if he should offer to keep in touch, but didn't know if that was appropriate or if the Persons would have any interest in speaking to him again. *Maybe we won't be Christmas card acquaintances, but would it be rubbing it in their faces that I lived while their son didn't?*

"Have a good life, Javier."

"Goodbye."

Agent Yang said what she needed to and they hung up. They made three more calls with similar outcomes.

Not all the family members had such a positive response to Javier's survival, and he understood the resentment. With each call Javier's gut clenched a little less when he said the words 'I killed him.' He clearly had some decisions to make, because none of families wanted a portion of the money. They had one last call to make. Then he planned on getting a stiff drink. Maybe he'd even call Malaki and see if he'd finished his shopping.

They dialed the number of a family in Chicago and waited for it to connect.

"I told you to stop calling here!"

Javier whipped his head towards Agent Yang.

"Mrs. Caballero, I won't take up much of your time. However, there is—"

"No, there's no however. I told you that we don't have a daughter."

Agent Yang sighed. "Mrs. Caballero, we already have a positive identification based on the information you provided when you reported your daughter missing."

"That pervert you found was not my daughter. My little girl would never do those disgusting things."

"Ma'am, I won't profess to understand what you're going through. I do have some information that might be welcome."

He glanced at Agent Yang and she shrugged. She'd warned him that this particular family had not reacted well to the news of their daughter's death. But unlike most of the loved ones she'd encountered in her career, it wasn't the woman's death that seemed to be the source of pain, but the information about her being a submissive. They'd already agreed before the call that Agent Yang would do the talking, so Javier sat back and listened.

"We did discover that Mr. Pesano had placed all the assets of his victims into a single account and we're notifying the families that they can contact the bank if they wish to make a claim."

There was a hesitation and unfortunately Javier wasn't surprised by the mercenary nature of humanity.

"Well, since that woman wasn't my daughter, then I guess I have no right to claim any of the money."

"That would be true." She looked at Javier and he nodded. "If, however, you want to change your mind, I'll leave the information with you."

He'd taken Tyler's advice and put the money into a trust. If any of the families wanted to claim part of the money, they'd contact Wilhelm. The Synder Foundation was generously willing to pay the attorney's retaining fee for the next year, the deadline they'd established for any claims to be made. While he'd spoken on the phone today he'd been very careful not to divulge any personal information. And, fortunately, so far his name had been kept out of the news reports.

They hung up the phone and Javier buried his face in his hands. People grieved in different ways, but he'd never understood why someone would turn their back on another person simply for one aspect of their personal lives. *Why does it continue to make a difference who and how a person loves? Isn't it more important in life that people find love at all?*

"Are you okay?" Agent Yang asked.

He scrubbed his face then opened his eyes. "Yeah. I mean in the grand scheme of things, I'm doing fine. So I guess I need to really start thinking about what I'm going to do with the money."

"You know, if I wasn't so good at my job, I would have thought I had the wrong person when I first met Mrs. Caballero. When we first made contact with her and her husband, it played out like so many times before. Too many times before. But the moment they found out she'd been a member of a BDSM club, they completely disavowed any knowledge of her. It sounds coldhearted, but I thought the money might make them reconsider. Their daughter has the right to be remembered with love and respect, not derision because she just happened to need something they don't understand."

"She will be. You and I will remember her. Her family in the community will remember her. There was a time when I thought losing the love of *mis abuelos y mi madre* would be the worst thing imaginable. That's part of the reason that I was such an unmitigated asshole in high school. I was so convinced that if I was honest about being gay, then my life would be over. It was only after I accepted those parts of myself I found a way out of the toxicity. Maybe she was lucky enough to find out the same before she died."

"I hope so. Based on what you've said during this process, I took the liberty of pulling together a list of organizations that support victims of violence. You can investigate which ones you want to donate to and how much to give away. Look, I understand a little bit about survivors' guilt, and you can't let it rule your life any more than that monster whose whip and brands scarred your skin."

He locked gazes with Agent Yang and for the first time saw layers of humanity beneath the shell of professionalism. There was the same expression in her eyes that he saw each morning in the mirror.

"I was on patrol with my squad in the Kunduz Province when we were ambushed by Taliban forces. Our combat controller was killed almost immediately and I used his radio to contact the Air Force to call in airstrikes. Sometimes I can still feel the heat of the explosions as they landed only feet away. We pressed deeper into the village but became trapped in an alley after running into a locked metal gate. Enemy forces fired machine guns and grenades at our position, killing five of my team members. Eventually a QRF team managed to evacuate us, but the smell of blood and burning buildings never really leaves. After I got home from deployment, I left the Army and joined the FBI."

"And now you stop a very different kind of monster."

"Or try to, anyway. Somedays we're better at it than others. Sometimes we're too late."

"That just means you're human. Thank you, Agent Yang, for everything."

They stood and Javier held out his hand.

She shook it, smiling. "Take care of yourself, Mr. Alde."

* * * *

"It's a pleasure to meet you, Dr. Alde."

"You as well, Dr. Davis. Thank you for asking me to come in."

He was as nervous as a new graduate going for his first job interview. The only difference was that he had a much nicer quality suit that was cut to fit his new leaner physique.

"I thought we'd sit down and talk for a little while, then I could introduce you to the team and show you around the facilities."

"Sounds perfect."

As they walked towards the manager's office, Javier took a few glances around. He was comfortable in the space and it seemed as though they had good quality equipment. He was surprised by the size of the offices. In his previous jobs, the therapist admin space had been little more than a glorified phone booth.

"Have a seat. So, your résumé indicates that you were the chief therapist in your prior position, but are now applying for a non-management position. That's generally the opposite of professionals who're still in the early years of their career."

"I can see why that may seem confusing. As I said on the phone, I took a leave of absence for personal reasons."

"Why did you decide not to return to your previous job?"

He'd been answering questions like this since he'd started his job search. He'd gotten various levels of reactions to his rehearsed response, but no job offers. And there was really no way to know for sure if his explanations were the reason, but there was always just some little look in the interviewer's eyes. It was as if their minds were closed to the idea of Javier joining the team and the rest of the interview was simply a curtesy.

Maybe it's the moment to lay it all on the line. He swallowed and tried very hard not to squirm in his chair.

"It was complicated. As you know, that particular facility is a subsidiary of Vista Rehab. While I was gone, the controlling partners promoted another employee to my position and now that I'm able to return to work, there's no longer a place for me."

Dr. Davis frowned and Javier saw the question in his eyes. What he'd just said sounded as though it went against every principle of FMLA regulations. From his first impressions and background research, this particular company felt like a good fit. He liked that it was actually owned by physical therapists and not a corporate figurehead who had no clinical experience.

"I can see the question in your eyes. I will say there are absolutely no hard feelings between me and my former employer. In fact, I've been going there for therapy as part of my recovery from ACL repair."

"Was the injury the reason for your leave of absence?"

"Not directly."

Time to put my money where my mouth is.

Javier sighed. He was either going to get another polite *we'll call when we've made a decision* and have his résumé thrown in the trash before he walked out of the door, or he might be sitting across from someone who understood that he just needed a chance to start over.

"Okay, here's the deal. Last October I was abducted and held prisoner by a man who tortured me for seven months. Now I'm at a point where I'm ready both physically and mentally to get my life back on track. I'm two weeks away from my level two sport test, but confident enough in my recovery to take on patients again. I'm a good therapist. I work hard, I enjoy the challenging cases and working in a team environment while maintaining my own autonomy."

"Well, that wasn't on the list of things I expected to hear today. I was already impressed with your experience and the references you submitted, but I have to say that I now admire you as an individual. Look,

I'm not going to drag out this process. This interview was really just a formality in my mind to make sure we didn't have some major personality clash." He slid a folder across his desk. "Here are the details about salary and benefits."

"Thank you. I'll review the information and give you my answer in a couple of days."

"Excellent. Let's go take a spin around the building and meet the others. I know I'm a bit biased, but I think we have a good crew. We support one another both in the office and out, often texting each other after hours and usually not about anything related to work."

"I like that. We had a talented crew where I was before, but our relationship stopped at the end of the day."

Javier took a critical examination of the facility. He liked that, like his old job, this practice specialized in sports and spine rehabilitation. There was nothing wrong with helping a little lady named Viola get off her walker after a hip replacement, but he thrived when presented with the opportunity to help a person learn to walk again after traumatic injury. He smiled as he saw his favorite anti-gravity treadmill. That thing had helped him make amazing progress during his recovery.

"Greg, this is Javier. He's considering joining the team."

"Nice to meet you." Greg held out his hand.

"You too. What do you like about working here?"

"Oh, nothing like going for the jugular. I think what I like best is that everyone here respects one another's strengths. We work hard, but like to have fun too."

"Glad to hear it." Javier nodded towards the laptop sitting on the exam table. "I see that you use the SerPT system. What do you think about it?"

"The LOT program remains cumbersome, despite recent improvements. Otherwise no complaints. You've used it before?"

"Yeah. We switched to that after we got tired of the nightmare with ProGen."

Greg groaned. "Oh, let me tell you about the time, back when I was working for a hospital in Austin, I had over two years' worth of documents pending approval because I didn't know that after you scan them into a chart, you have to sign off on them."

"Ouch. Well, maybe we can share more war stories another time."

Greg nodded. "Nice to meet you."

The facilities were much nicer in person than the pictures he'd seen on the web, and first impressions of the other employees gave him a sense that they could be friends. All that was really left was to review the salary and benefit information. On one hand, he really needed the job, but on the other he had enough respect for himself and his skills that he wasn't willing to accept a subpar offer.

* * * *

An hour later he knocked on Malaki's door. He hadn't texted ahead, so he hoped his friend was home, and if he was home, wasn't entertaining a certain tall blond with a swimmer's body and tempting blue eyes. Jaxon was a perfectly nice guy, but every time the three of them were together Javier just wanted to impotently growl like a Chihuahua guarding its food.

He raised his hand to knock one more time, since he'd seen Malaki's truck in the parking lot. The door swung open and he came face to face with Malaki's massive tattoo. Beads of water cascaded over the Samoan design that Javier might have imagined tracing with his tongue on occasion. The saliva pooling in his mouth got lodged in his throat when Malaki stood there in nothing but a towel. However, the pleasure fog in his brain lifted when he spied the neighbor sitting on the sofa just behind Malaki, looking very much at home.

"Javier!"

"Sorry, I didn't mean to interrupt. I'll call you later."

He turned to leave and the acid that bubbled in his gut threatened to spew all over the walkway leading to Malaki's front door.

"Wait, wait! What's up? Are you okay?"

"Yeah. I just. The job is mine if I want it, and I thought…." He shrugged.

Malaki rushed forward and threw his arms around Javier. "Fuck, yeah. I knew you could do it!"

Holy fuck. Holy fuck. Holy fuck. There is a huge, hot, nearly naked man pressed up against me.

Javier leaned in, inhaling the scent of Malaki's soap. His fingers itched to dig into the muscles covering the man's back, but the sound of someone clearing their throat froze him in his tracks. Malaki spun around and the towel slipped dangerously low. As Javier reached to save Malaki's decency, his fingers ended up brushing the curve of the man's spine. Muscles twitched and Malaki stiffened.

"Jaxon, Javier got the job! Isn't that great!"

"Congrats. I know it's a nice day and all, but unless you want your other neighbors to really get to know you, maybe this little gathering should be moved indoors."

Malaki tightened his grip on his towel. "You're right. Come on, Javier. We'll go get drinks to celebrate."

He looked between Malaki and Jaxon. Jaxon's frown took over his face. Even though the two men were not involved, clearly the blond had developed some feelings for Malaki and was hoping to take their friendship to the next level. If he were a better man, he would step away, but he was just enough of a selfish bastard that he wasn't willing to simply hand over Malaki.

"Sounds good." He put his hand on Malaki's back to guide him towards his front door. His skin was warm and firm. Sweat beaded up beneath Javier's suit, and it wasn't from the heat outside.

They entered Malaki's condo, which looked much more lived-in lately. Having furniture made a big difference. Javier had firsthand knowledge of just how comfortable the large overstuffed pieces Malaki had chosen were.

"I'm going to get dressed, then we can head out to Sinclair's and grab some cold ones."

Malaki disappeared into his bedroom and instead of Jaxon watching the miles of muscled, tattooed skin, he was watching Javier. He slipped his hands into the pockets of his suit and met the Jaxon's gaze.

"Didn't mean to burst in on the two of you."

"Hmm, but not gracious enough to leave."

"Was there a reason to? Malaki's never mentioned that the two of you were anything but friendly neighbors."

Malaki came out of the room dressed, but the sight was no less pleasing. Javier really needed to figure out what he wanted, or not so much what he wanted but what he was going to do about these feelings that kept inconveniently churning inside him. If he wasn't going to stake a claim, then he really did need to step aside.

"Let's go. We can take my truck."

Chapter Eight

Malaki leaned a little harder on Javier as they made their way along the balcony to his front door. He really wasn't that buzzed, but it gave him an excuse to get closer to the man. To feel Javier's body pressed up against his. Earlier, when he'd hugged Javier outside, it had almost become an embarrassing moment as his cock had nearly made a tent of his towel. He'd been holding back on his feelings, unwilling to push Javier and scare the man off after everything he'd been through. But it had become painfully clear that if their relationship was going to move to the next level, it was going to be up to him. They got to his front door and he dug his keys out of his pocket.

"It's late. You want to stay over?" Was it his imagination or did Javier press against his back as he opened the door?

"I shouldn't."

Malaki chuckled. "I shouldn't have had that last drink, but it seemed like such a good idea at the time."

He opened the door and the two of them walked inside. Jaxon had declined to come home with them, saying he had a group of friends that had texted, wanting to meet up. Malaki got the feeling his neighbor had picked up on the tension between him and Javier.

He stood in his dark living room. Javier shut the door and Malaki found it harder to breathe. It only took a few steps and he had Javier's back against the wall. Javier dug his fingers into Malaki's chest and his eyes were wide open, but Malaki didn't sense any fear radiating from him.

"What are you doing?" Javier asked, softly.

"What I've wanted to do for ages."

"You're drunk. People regret things they do when they're drunk."

Malaki leaned in and skimmed his lips against Javier's neck. "I'm not really drunk. I just wanted to get you back up here." His hands shook as he slid them inside Javier's suit coat. "You look so fucking hot in this suit. All night I've imagined stripping each layer off, one by one. I've thought of doing that lots of times."

Shivers ran through him at Javier's exhalation of breath against his skin.

"I nearly passed out when I saw you in nothing but that towel earlier. But I don't know about this, Mal. Don't get me wrong, I'm attracted to you. I've imagined…a lot. But I don't… I can't trust myself."

"Is that what's been holding you back?"

Javier nodded and sighed when Malaki grazed his temple with his lips.

"Then don't trust yourself. Trust me. What you had with those others isn't us. You're not the same person you were, and I'm most certainly not some psychopath."

"I… I should tell you more about all that."

"And I'll listen. When you're ready. For tonight I want to touch you, maybe share a few kisses."

"You think I should trust the man who manipulated me into his home?"

Malaki froze and realized he'd made a serious tactical error. Here he'd waited to make a move because he knew Javier was skittish about starting a relationship, then the first thing he'd done was to manipulate the man.

Javier cupped Malaki's cheek. "Sorry, bad joke. I'm a little nervous. It's not just the trust thing. I… I've never been in this situation before."

He cradled Javier's hand and led him over to the sofa. Javier started to take off his suit coat, but Malaki stopped him. "Let me?" He walked around and rested his hands on Javier's shoulders. The scent of Javier's cologne drifted up and teased his senses. They were really going to do this after so many months. He rested his chin on the top of Javier's head, savoring the moment, then slid his jacket off. The warmth of Javier's skin through his shirt made Malaki's fingers tingle with the need to explore, but he needed to take one step at a time. He tossed the suit coat onto a chair, then they sat side by side. Typically, the sofa allowed them to spread out while they kicked back and watched a game or movie. But, tonight, Malaki made sure to sit right next to Javier. The moment he sat and took Javier's hand, his body settled comfortably. Javier, on the other hand, was twitchier than muscles hooked up to an electro-stim machine.

"Talk to me."

"Let's just say that in all my previous relationships I was…in charge, and back there I was…not."

"Mmm, are we talking you tend to be a little bossy or —"

"I was a Dom. That's how I met Luca. The man who took me."

"He was another? Like you?"

"No, he was pretending to be a submissive."

"I know there's more to this story, but for our immediate situation, are you telling me that you'd feel more comfortable if *you* held *me* up against the wall?"

"I don't know anymore," Javier whispered.

"Then how about we figure out what we want together? Right now, I'd really like to kiss you. Can I do that?"

Javier tilted his head up and Malaki took that as permission. He slid his thumb across Javier's lower lip. Warm breath moistened Javier's skin. Seated as they were, Javier's head only came up to his shoulder. Malaki lowered his head inch by inch. Javier had made no mention of any sexual trauma as part of his ordeal, but he wasn't willing to take anything for granted.

Malaki brushed his lips against Javier's for a moment. Time froze and his heart stilled until Javier leaned in again. He could have captured Javier's lips and devoured the man, but instead Malaki held still. Javier slid his hands up Malaki's chest and around his neck. He pulled down and brought their mouths together again. It was everything he'd imagined kissing Javier would be, and so much more. His heart raced and his skin burned where they touched. But it was a burn he would gladly suffer, because the pleasure far outweighed the pain.

"Javi," he whispered.

"I like that. I've always been Sir or Master. It was something I expected, I felt was deserved, but never made me catch my breath like the sound of my name on your lips."

He gathered his man in his arms and merged their mouths together in a slow exploration.

Javier couldn't remember a time when he'd kissed a man simply for the pleasure of doing so. For so many years, kisses had been either a means to an end or a power play. Something to give his subs as a reward. But kissing Malaki was an experience that had no ulterior motive other than sharing touch and taste.

They shifted their bodies on the couch and Javier ended up on his back with Malaki above him. He stiffened.

"I'm sorry. Here, let me —"

"No, no. It's okay. Just gut reaction, but you actually feel..." He squirmed a little and wrapped his arms around Malaki. "I think I like it."

"I think I like it too, but I will confess most of the guys I've been with have always assumed that I like taking charge all the time."

"When I sought out play partners, I always looked for men who were bigger than me. There was something about getting a man whose appearance screamed uber-alpha to bend to my will that really pumped blood to my cock. One who looked like he could bench-press a small car, but became a puddle when I fucked him." He smoothed out Malaki's frown. "I can see the questions swirling around in your head, but I don't have the answers yet."

"We can just take it one question at a time."

Javier pulled Malaki down while arching up against his larger body. He was certain that his past patterns had been a psychological ploy with himself to see if he had what it took to earn the submission of a man who could physically overpower him. Lying beneath Malaki was a drastic role reversal for him, but Javier was determined to shut off his brain and ride the wave of desire reawakening his body.

"You know, I really wasn't sure this was possible anymore."

Malaki nibbled on Javier's neck as he opened the button on his collar. "What's that?"

Javier arched his hips, throbbing their erections together. "I haven't been able to maintain any kind of hard-on since my escape."

Malaki sat up and pulled Javier with him. "I haven't asked you anything about what happened because I wanted you to feel comfortable enough to share with me. As your friend, I'm here to support you. As something more, I'm hoping to help you heal."

"I appreciate that, and I want you to know that I haven't been purposely holding back from you. I've been seeing a therapist to help me work through my issues."

"I'm glad."

"Sorry, my little comment killed the mood."

"There's nothing to apologize for. I just want to make sure that even though we're working things out as we go, I don't stumble on some kind of painful situation."

Javier wiped his hands on his pants. "My body went through a lot of trauma. Some of which you know, since you read my medical reports, but none of the torture I endured involved sexual abuse. My therapist feels that my recent issues are more mental than physical."

"Hmm, well, I've always been a big supporter of continuing your therapy program at home. Wait. That sounds weird."

Javier chuckled. "That's okay. I get it. And you are the best therapist I've ever worked with. So you want to design a program for me? You can personally supervise my progress."

"Now those are some goals I look forward to achieving."

Chapter Nine

Javier studied his tablet with his first patient's chart information. He was seeing a high school pitcher who'd recently undergone Tommy John surgery. The occurrence of the ligament repair procedure had dramatically increased in the last several years. Some people chalked it up to awareness from the media, others that the improvement in imaging caught the injury earlier. In Javier's opinion, kids were throwing too hard and too much at ages when their bodies were not prepared for the strain.

The notes indicated that this particular young man had already caught the eye of a couple of major league teams. As a former athlete who'd earned his college degree as a result of his ability to race down the grid iron, Javier could understand the almost panic-inducing desire to rehab as quickly as possible to get back on the field.

"You good to go?" Davis popped his head around the corner of his office door.

"Yep. It's funny, I thought I would be nervous, just until I get that first one under my belt, you know? But I can't stop smiling."

"Feel a little bit like coming home after a long trip?"

"Yeah, I guess." The door opened and a young man in an arm sling walked in. "Showtime!"

Davis gave him a thumbs-up. The young man's father stood behind him and appeared to be studying the facility, no doubt assessing whether they were up to the job of getting his player back on the field.

"Hi, I'm Dr. Alde. You must be Francisco."

"Hey, what's up?"

The kid had quite a deep mature voice, but still that sullen monotone quality of a teenager.

"Frank, manners."

He looked over at his father and Javier practically heard the internal sarcastic dialogue rolling around the kid's head.

Ah, teenagers.

"Come this way and we'll start your intake assessment. Mr. Martinez, if you'd like to have a seat in the waiting area? We have some comfortable chairs with a TV, refreshments, a work area if you need it and iPads with e-zines and other games."

"Sweet. Wish all the doctors' offices had been like that," Francisco said.

"It is a very nice set-up. In my experience, there's nothing worse than having to go to the doctor and being forced to wait next to a stranger who can't stop coughing, while battling a migraine and angsting over deadlines back at the office, or in your case maybe your ERA and how you're going to manage getting that cutter down in the zone."

Francisco laughed, and Javier thought he'd managed to establish a good rapport with the kid. He was here to work and help his patients get back to their daily activity level, but nowhere was it written in the physical therapist handbook that he couldn't be friendly. There was an art to the balance between being professional and casual with patients.

"I don't know. Maybe I should be with my son, at least initially. What if you have questions?"

"I totally understand if that would make you more comfortable." Francisco was clearly old enough to be alone in an appointment, but Dad seemed to need his hovering rights. "We will be in this first cube, so if I do need any information I can easily come ask."

"Dad, I'll be fine. This isn't my first time in PT."

"Okay, okay. I do have some emails to return."

"Great! This way, Francisco."

"You can call me Paco. Everyone on the team does."

It was good that the kid was still thinking in terms of team environment. If he'd given up on his dream of pitching in the big leagues, he'd probably do everything to avoid the association with baseball.

Javier led him into the curtained-off cubicle that they used for assessments and treatments that required some privacy. He really liked that about his new job. Most rehab facilities were just one big room with scattered tables and equipment. As a provider, he hadn't thought much about it, but now, having been a patient too, he understood how having everyone being able to watch his progress or lack thereof had been uncomfortable.

"So tell me about your game. What pitches do you have? What's your top speed?"

"I've got a solid four and two seam fastball in the low nineties, and lefties can't catch up with my curveball. I'd just started working on a cutter when this happened."

"That's awesome. Well, I'm going to do my best to get you back on the mound for next season."

"You really think it's possible?"

"The surgical report indicates that everything went as well as possible. If you maintain your rehab schedule and things are progressing well, I don't see why you can't start throwing in the spring."

The kid teared up a little. It was as though he'd been putting up a good front for his parents and teammates, but the worry had been slowly eating him up deep inside. Javier understood the feeling.

"Look, I recently had to go through my own rehab for knee injury. My playing days are over, but I'm far from the point in my life when I anticipate nothing more than sitting in my recliner. I'm going to lay it on the line. This is not going to be easy. You're going to hurt, sweat, probably cry and even hate me a little before we're done. But I promise not to give up on you if you promise not to give up on yourself."

"I can work with that. What do we do first?"

* * * *

Javier took a sip of his drink and sighed. A pleasant warmth from the tequila rushed through his bloodstream. The noise from the crowd at Zandy's wasn't so overwhelming that he, Brandon, Tyler and Malaki couldn't enjoy their conversation. He hadn't told Brandon and Tyler about the change in his and Malaki's relationship, but given the looks Brandon had been throwing his way for the past twenty minutes, the man was picking up a shift in the current. It was fun to torment him a little, and see how long they could go before the question was blurted out.

"So how was your first day?" Brandon asked.

"Felt good. It was really nice to use my brain for something other than daily function requirements. I thought I might feel a bit rusty, even after reviewing procedures and the latest research for the past couple of weeks, but the day went smoothly. The facilities are great and the people seem cool so far."

"That's good. I know you were eager to get back, but I imagine there had to be just a few nerves."

"How did the knee hold up?" Malaki asked.

"Good. Had a couple of twinges here and there if I wasn't paying attention and moved weird, but I didn't have any problem with mobility or stability."

He straightened his leg to let Malaki give a quick assessment of the tenderness and effusion he'd reported having after being on his feet all day. Malaki placed his hand on Javier's knee under the table, and the warmth of his palm through his slacks made Javier wish he was in shorts so he could feel those work-roughed fingers on his bare skin. The caress was simultaneously intimate and clinical. When Malaki continued to slide his hand up Javier's thigh, the backs of his fingers grazed Javier's balls and he swallowed, trying to subtly shift in his seat.

He leaned over and placed his lips next to Javier's ear, saying softly, "I still think you need to ice it tonight when you get home."

"You keep that up and my knee won't be the only thing needing ice tonight."

"So this is a thing now?" Tyler asked.

Javier smiled and looked at Malaki. "Told you he'd crack first."

Malaki gestured for their server. "Round of drinks on me this time."

Javier gazed across the table to assess his best friends' reactions. Brandon, as usual, wore a mask worthy of the greatest poker player. Tyler's eyes were truly the windows to his soul, which right now were cloudy enough that Javier's view was obscured.

"Yes, this is a thing."

"How long?"

"Not very. And before the question can even pop into your nosy little minds, we're taking it slowly, figuring out exactly what we want."

Tyler looked at Malaki. "So you know?"

"About his past relationships? Yes. About everything that happened? As he's willing to share."

Tyler held up his glass. "Well, then, I, for one, am glad."

He found himself holding his breath as Brandon stayed silent. Javier still had some reservations about starting a relationship with Malaki. Was he really ready? Did he have enough trust in himself to read and respond to their interactions without falling back on bad habits? It was as if he was walking through dense fog, unsure of his next step, but he knew he had to keep moving. If he stood still and let the mist consume him, he'd never find his way to being whole again. It had been Brandon's and Tyler's hands that had led him towards the right path, but maybe, just maybe, it would be Malaki's deep voice that acted as the beacon for the next leg of his journey.

"Give me one adjective that describes Javier?" Brandon asked Malaki.

It was a simple question, but really spoke volumes about how a man thought and acted in the world.

Malaki took Javier's hand and laced their fingers together. "Resilient."

"Hmm…."

He glanced over at Brandon. The man's lack of response had made Javier's blood pressure rise a good ten points in the last five minutes. Would Brandon support him and Malaki? Did he deserve that support or had he burned too many karma-bridges over the years? And if he didn't have Brandon's support, would he have the fortitude to stay and work on this budding relationship? He turned to study Malaki. The man looked like a fierce warrior with his large ink designs, layers of muscles, and a frame that towered over the common man. But Javier had seen the depth of his person in moments when he'd been ready to give up during therapy. Malaki had been the one to make him believe he could do it. It had been Malaki's voice giving him strength to continue when Javier's body was ready to give out from the pain and exertion. And now that he'd recovered on a physical level, he hungered to hear Malaki's voice in the dark with much more explicit and intimate demands.

"Yes."

He jerked his gaze back towards Brandon. "What?"

"Yes. I agree that is a good word to describe you. Of course, I would have also accepted pig headed, opinionated, ambitious, charismatic or intelligent."

"Thanks. I think?"

The server brought their dinner selections and Javier inhaled the spices floating up from his green chili lasagna. While he looked forward to stuffing his face with the pasta, Malaki had been true to form and ordered the Texas Gulf Redfish, and the grilled squash, zucchini and sun-dried tomatoes did look delicious.

"So the two of you have some shindig this weekend for Tyler's family?" Javier asked

"The Crystal Charity Ball is tomorrow night. It's the last big event of the season, and while I gratefully let my parents and brother handle a lot of the obligations for the family corporation and foundations, there're a few I make it a point to attend each year. This year Brandon and I attended the TACA Fiftieth Anniversary Gala and the Two x Two for Aids Art Gala and Auction."

"It's just a good thing that all these events are after foaling season and things are quieter on the ranch. I tried to talk him into going to the Cattle Barons' Ball this year, but no such luck. He promised me next year though."

"We all know you have a thing for cowboys, but since when are you a country music fan?" Javier asked.

Brandon smiled up at Tyler, his very own cowboy, and Javier practically started to sweat with the heat being generated between his two friends. It was as if the they were able to share a thousand words in a few seconds.

I wonder if Mal and I will ever get to that point?

Being that absolutely open to another person was slightly terrifying, but at the same time to have a connection on that intimate a level was a rarely seen miracle. *Speaking of connections, it's getting a little squirm-inducing on this side of the booth.* He whistled to catch Brandon and Tyler's attention.

"Hmm?" Brandon asked. "Oh, sorry. I'm not really. But I hear it's an amazing party, and a great people-watching event."

"I can't really imagine going to stuff like that. How do you relate to anyone? I mean, the two of you just seem so normal and anytime I've seen pictures or read about society stuff, it's like those who go live on another planet compared to the rest of us plebeians."

Tyler shrugged. "I've never known any different, but my grandfather made sure I kept both my feet firmly planted in the dirt."

Brandon shrugged. "I used to think like that when we first started dating. Do you remember that first event you took me to at The Texas Hall of State? There I was in my rented tux, trying to act like I mingled with millionaires every day, while the whole time inside I was screeching like a teenage girl about to be devoured by Jaws."

"Seriously?" Tyler asked.

Brandon nodded. "Anyway, after a couple more soirees, I figured out there are some people who are elitist douchebags and others who are actually fun to hang with despite the fact that they have a lot of money."

"That's true. I mean, I come from money, but I chose to run a ranch and horse breeding program. So in the eyes of a few, I don't belong, but they're not willing to risk insulting my family to say anything."

The four of them finished their supper and by the time their plates had been cleared away, Javier's body temperature was climbing from more than just the chilies. Malaki paid for Javier's meal, and even though he could have paid for his own meal at this point, the gesture was not lost on him. It was again unfamiliar territory, but didn't chafe at his instincts in any way.

They stood outside the restaurant and Javier slipped his hand into Malaki's. He received a soft squeeze in turn and couldn't stop the dopey grin that crept across his face, no doubt making him appear rather simple.

"Well, you kids behave. Do we need to have a talk about being safe?" Brandon teased.

Javier swallowed and the delicious meal he'd just finished suddenly churned in his gut. He couldn't seem to focus and his heart raced. Bile threatened to erupt in a rather unpleasant display of nature's force. His legs shook and he had a brief moment of consciousness when it occurred to him that he was about to experience another dose of pain, but couldn't get his limbs to coordinate enough to stop the collapse of his body.

Warmth enveloped him and instead of the harsh ringing sound in his ears, he heard a mellow rumble. Vibrations against his cheek seemed to stimulate his muscles into working as a team to translate the random neurons firing from his brain into meaningful movement.

"What?"

"That's it. Focus on my voice, Javi. Look at me and only me."

He blinked and Malaki's face swam into focus. His worried gaze trained on Javier and the light from the exterior of the restaurant gleamed off his shaved head. He fell into Malaki's dark eyes. How was it that on one man that shade could emote darkness and in another almost a radiant warmth?

"Shit. I am so sorry, Javier," Brandon said.

He looked around and was relieved to find that it was still just the four of them. The last thing Javier wanted was to become the object of every patron's Instagram feed. He sat up and shook off the last of the clouds in his brain. Spying Brandon and Tyler standing just to his left, he held out his hand to Brandon, who pulled him up.

"What are you sorry for?"

"I was just giving you guys shit and then, I don't know…clearly I said something and you just disappeared."

"Well, it wasn't your fault. Clearly some rubber band in my brain just got twanged the wrong way and snapped. My therapist said we still don't understand all the triggers that might ignite a reaction after my experience. It could be a sound or a smell—who knows?"

"Do you have flashbacks often?" Tyler asked.

Javier shook his head. "They're not flashbacks. Not really. More like I just kind of go absent. And it's only happened a handful of times."

Malaki rubbed small circles on his back. "A protective shell. A way to shield your mind from whatever is happening in reality. You've said that there are gaps in your memory during your time in captivity. Maybe something similar?"

"Maybe. Sorry for being such a drama queen. Can we just forget this happened and say have a good night?"

Tyler came forward and gave Javier a hug. "Have a good night? Absolutely. Forget and not worry about my friend? Not going to happen."

Javier sniffed and tried to hide the emotions that threatened to bubble up.

"Group hug!" Brandon yelled as his arms came around Javier from behind.

He let out a grunt as Malaki joined the melee. "All right, who touched my ass?"

"Don't look at me," Brandon said. "My hands are up here."

Javier glanced over his shoulder and grinned evilly. "I didn't say it was a hand."

"Oh please, your ass is locked up tighter than Fort Knox." Brandon said as he backed away and ran over to Tyler's side.

"Maybe I've just been waiting for the guy with the right-size key?"

Both Brandon and Tyler's jaws fell open. It took everything in him to hold in a laugh.

Malaki captured Javier's waist and pulled him into the circle of his arms. "It might take hours, but even the most stubborn locks release with the right touch."

"Umm, okay, so have a good night, guys!" Javier said as he spun around, commandeered Malaki's hand and dragged him towards the parking lot.

Tyler and Brandon's laughter followed them, but with Malaki's huge paw in his grip and his thundering steps hot on Javier's heels, he couldn't have cared less about the future ribbing he was sure to receive. They reached Malaki's big truck and Javier used his momentum to fling the big man around and put his back to the passenger-side door.

He knew that Malaki had let Javier manhandle him. He had no illusions that he was stronger than the Samoan. One thing he and Malaki had figured out was that Javier was still bossy, but the exertion of control had a very different dynamic nowadays. He ground his mouth against Malaki's, but instead of the urge to pin the man's hands immobile, he savored the passion and determination behind Mal's touch.

Malaki had a strong grip on the back of Javier's shirt and he arched up to plaster their bodies closer together. His cock found its way to half-mast, which was still a feeling that he reveled in as a personal accomplishment. It seemed as though he wasn't alone in his excitement, judging by the detailed map Malaki was making of his body.

It was difficult to slam on the brakes now that he'd finally gotten his motor running, but Javier knew this wasn't the time.

"Want to go back to my place?" Malaki asked.

"Yes." He backed up a step and a breeze blew between them, cooling more than just their bodies.

Malaki smiled but didn't move away from the truck. "It's okay."

Javier shook his head. "No, it's not. Part of me really wants to go back to your place and fuck. I want to see that glorious body of yours bared to the moonlight and run my tongue along every one of those lines inked into your skin."

"And the other part?"

"Is scared absolutely shitless that I won't really know what to do once we get there. I've been having sex one way for a long time."

"Let me ask you a question. Do you still crave having a submissive under your command?"

Javier let go of Malaki and leaned back against the truck. He closed his eyes and pictured himself back in some of the more aggressive scenes he'd participated in. Images of cock and ball cages made him cringe. The idea of using a flogger or even giving a man a hard spanking made his semi disappear. Then he pictured Malaki on his knees, as he would previously have required all scenes to begin. He moaned as frustration engulfed him.

"Don't think, just feel," Malaki whispered into his ear.

Instead of focusing on scenes, he imagined how it would be to have Malaki nip his way across Javier's flesh. The sensation of sheets rubbing against his skin as their bodies rolled across a bed. Not him conducting a scene, but two men sharing the experience of making love.

"No. I don't want to command you."

Malaki ran his hand up Javier's face and turned his head till they were facing each other again. "While I have to admit you really sent my wheels spinning when you shoved me up against the truck, I'm not wired to be somebody's boy."

"I don't need a boy. I need a partner. I mean not in the sense that I'm about to pop the question, but I need somebody who's my equal."

Malaki lowered his head and even though Javier knew he was about to be kissed, he tilted his head away so he could whisper in Mal's ear, "Um, there is one thing that hasn't changed from my old days."

Malaki pressed his forehead against Javier's and whispered, "What's that?"

"I want to be the one to fuck you."

"Oh, I think that is very doable. I've ached to feel you inside me for months now."

Javier shivered and his cock hardened with the anticipation of sliding into Malaki's tight heat. "Get your ass in this truck now," he growled.

The ride back to Malaki's condo seemed to stretch on forever. The distance wasn't great, but with each mile Javier's inner monologue kept alternating between, *'God I hope I can still do this'* and *'Oh my God, this is so exciting!'* If he hadn't been assured by his therapist that he was doing quite well, he'd have been concerned about developing some kind of split personality disorder.

Malaki braked hard as they pulled up outside his complex. Javier turned to look at his soon-to-be lover, but the man was already out of the door and his long strides were eating away at the distance between the parking lot and his front door.

"Well, okay, then."

Javier fought with the seatbelt, and was seconds away from gnawing through the damn thing when the latch finally released. He jumped out and slammed the door closed. The race to the steps outside Malaki's condo made his heart rate jump, but the sight of his man standing at the top of the stairs with laser beams of lust burning from his eyes was what nearly gave him a heart attack.

Malaki was no sub and Javier knew that what was about to go down would shift his world onto yet another axis. He just hoped he'd survive again.

He stalked Malaki up the stairs. Step by step he closed the gap till he felt the heat radiating off Malaki's body.

"What are you waiting for?" he asked.

"Wanted to make sure you were okay. Didn't want your knee to give out with the mad dash you made across the courtyard."

"Saw that, did you?"

"Mmhm. Besides, I've got plans for that body of yours. Can't have you injuring yourself…again."

He reached up and pulled Malaki's head down till their lips were nearly a hair apart. "Well, it's a good thing I've got an in with the best PT in Dallas."

"You're about to get a lot more in him."

"Fuck yes, I am. Now move it. I find that my taste for public play isn't quite what it used to be. Only I get to see this gorgeous body of yours."

They quickly made their way down the balcony and as Malaki unlocked the door, Javier plastered himself against his lover's back. He gripped Malaki's hip with one hand and ran the other up his back beneath the shirt that had been tauntingly molded to his muscles all night.

"Hurry, Mal, my lips are tingling with the need to explore every inch of your body."

Malaki moaned and the door flew open. The glass rattled as it banged against the wall. As soon as they'd sealed themselves away from the outside world, Malaki ripped off his shirt. Even in the dark, the ink that decorated his body highlighted each curve and sinew.

"Holy fucking shit," Javier whispered.

Malaki was in the process of releasing the closure of his pants when Javier placed his hands on top, halting him.

"Let me."

Mal panted with each brush of Javier's fingers against his skin. He was just evil enough to tease the larger man with a lighter touch than they both craved, but the devil turned against him when Malaki tightened his abs and several hundred synapses in Javier's brain exploded at the sight of the muscles that Malaki could easily have used to overpower him, but instead remained cemented in front of him.

His fingers shook while he fumbled with the button and zipper of Malaki's pants, but finally the stubborn fasteners gave way and the slacks dropped to the floor.

All that hid the full glory of Malaki's body from him was a tight pair of boxer briefs.

"What in the hell is that?"

Malaki kicked off his pants, socks and shoes then stood facing Javier with his hands on his hips. "What?"

Javier pointed at the briefs. "That."

"If you have to ask, then you're rustier at this then I thought."

He jerked his head up, tearing his gaze away from the spectacle in front of him. Malaki's smile lit up the room, but still wasn't as bright as the glowing images decorating his underwear.

"Haven't you ever seen a cat riding a rainbow unicorn through outer space before?"

"Sorry, LSD is not on my list of medications. Those are ridiculous. You know that, right?"

"Sadly, they were a gag gift from my sister. I tried to hate them, but the damn things are just so comfortable. Now, are you going to keep asking questions about my underwear or can we move on to what's beneath them?"

Malaki started towards him and Javier became the prey in their little game. He took several steps back, thankful that Malaki kept an uncluttered home. He couldn't seem to look away from Malaki's eyes. It was so easy to visualize the primitive warriors of his lineage simmering beneath the surface of his cosmopolitan veneer. It wasn't until he saw the doorframe out of the corner of his eyes that he realized Malaki had herded him into the bedroom.

He shook off the lustful hypnosis and started to undo the buttons of his polo. He went to lift off his shirt, but stopped. A clammy sweat beaded on his body where moments ago he'd been about to burn up from desire.

"What's wrong?"

"I just realized that I'm about to be naked."

"That's generally how this works. I've done it quick and dirty a few times in my life when only the necessary bits were exposed, but that's not where I thought we wanted to take this."

"No, it's just that nobody's seen me naked since… I have scars. Lots of them. And not all of them are surgical."

Malaki froze. "What do you need?"

That was a question he didn't know how to answer. His scars didn't bother him, not really. Not in a way that many would assume. He didn't see them as weakness or badges of honor. They didn't make him feel particularly ugly, but he also knew they weren't exactly nice to look at. Some of them were still sensitive and irritating, but touching them didn't send him into a tailspin of flashbacks featuring how they'd been made. They were just there. But would they turn Malaki off? Would all their talk of being equal change once the other man was faced with the reality of Javier's imprisonment?

"I need them not to matter to you. But I have no right to ask that. And you really have no control over your thoughts and feelings."

"I can't say they won't matter to me, because *you* matter to me. But I will say that scars in any form will not define you in my eyes."

"Fair enough."

He whipped off his clothes as quickly as possible, stripping down to nothing, and presented himself for inspection. He stood tall, but couldn't help closing his eyes. His remaining senses told him that Malaki was near. The scent of his aftershave, the sound of his steps on the floor—the hairs on Javier's body stood up as he detected Malaki's approach.

"Can I touch you?"

He nodded, unsure of his voice

"Do you want me to keep the lights off?"

"I don't care."

Seconds of silence almost had him opening his eyes.

"Yes, you do. You're standing here waiting to hear my verdict, but hiding from me at the same time."

He's right, damn him. Javier swallowed and let Malaki in. All the way in.

"There you are," Malaki said, as he cupped Javier's face. "Eyes on me. See what I see. Hear what I say."

Malaki kissed him briefly, the touch so fleeting Javier would almost say it hadn't happened, but every time their lips touched, Javier was one hundred and ten percent aware of it. Malaki 's gaze zeroed in on the brand Luca had burned into his flesh over his left ribcage. He traced the raised lines then covered the scar tissue with his palm. The warmth of Malaki's hand soothed Javier like a heat pad on aching muscles. Mal gave the same treatment to the lines that crisscrossed his chest, abdomen and back from the whips. Javier gasped as Mal kissed the points where he'd been connected to electrocution cables.

"I'm glad the fucker is dead. The how and why each one happened doesn't matter. I'll listen if you want or need to talk about it, but all that really matters to me is that you're here, you're mine and we're looking toward the future together."

Whoa, that sounds really permanent, but not necessarily wrong.

"Get those stupid shorts off and get on the bed."

Malaki smiled. "Yes, sir."

That sounded so wrong coming from him, and Javier loved it because he still wanted Mal with every fiber of his being. It was freeing in a way, because in that moment he knew they could do this. He could be this man, *the* man for Malaki, without the fear that his old life was lurking in the background, whispering in his ear.

Chapter Ten

"Hand me two of those pillows then lift your ass."

He admired the glute bridge move that Malaki showed off then shoved the pillows beneath his hips, elevating his backside off the mattress.

"Now, spread your legs."

Javier heard the steel in his voice and took stock of the situation. He didn't think Malaki would mind him getting a little toppy. In fact, the man had said some aggressiveness turned him on. Javier smiled at the little hitch he heard in Malaki's breath. Smiling during sex was new to him and he found that he liked it. Mal bent his knees then spread his thighs, exposing himself.

"Where's your slick?"

"Where else would it be?"

Javier headed for the bedside, but stopped when he saw Mal holding up the tube.

"Stashed under the pillow from the last time I jacked off thinking about you."

He grabbed the lube and climbed onto the bed next to Malaki.

"Did you play with your ass, or just stroke your cock till you cried my name?" A sense of satisfaction overcame him when Mal's ass clenched. He got a good amount of lube on a couple of his fingers then circled the small opening that beckoned to him. "God, that's beautiful. I can't wait to get inside you."

"Then stop talking and —"

He plunged two fingers into Mal's channel, then stilled. Malaki's groan vibrated from deep within his body and up through Javier where they connected. Malaki bucked his hips, trying to achieve deeper penetration, but Javier held his hips still. The scowl that marred his man's expressive face made Javier's smile bigger.

"What's the matter, beautiful?"

"Your fingers are buried in my ass, and I thought we were finally getting somewhere, but now you've developed some kind of fuckalysis."

"Fuckalysis? Can you tell me what the ICD-10 code would be for that?"

"Are you kidding me?"

"What's the rush? Do you have someplace else to be?"

Javier pressed the bundle of nerves inside, and Mal's cry made Javier realize this was a level of control that he still relished.

"Fuck me, Javi," Malaki whispered.

He stroked the silky inner walls of Mal's channel, stretching him slowly. He continued to move his fingers, enjoying the heat and his quiet, needy sounds. Malaki's large form took over the entire center of the bed. Javier had just enough space next to him to get an up-close inspection of the cut muscles Mal worked so hard to maintain. The pillows beneath Mal's hips tilted his pelvis, allowing Javier easy access to his ass. Javier licked his lips at the sight of Mal's dick pointed toward the ceiling. The dark flesh was thick, just like the rest of him, and Javier swallowed the saliva that pooled with his anticipation of taking that cock deep in his throat. Mal didn't have much body hair, and Javier didn't know if that was by choice or due to his Polynesian ancestry. Either way, there was little to obscure his view of Mal's body with his legs spread wide and his knees slightly bent.

There was nothing delicate or slender in any strong swell or curve. Malaki was a modern-day warrior whose blood ran with the lineage of chiefs, but right then all that strength was laid out before Javier in supplication. Javier scissored his fingers, and Mal lifted his hips a fraction while his toes curled.

"Please…"

"Don't worry. We're getting there. Maybe a little reward is in order for being so good and letting me explore your tight ass."

Mal's cock head gleamed with pre-cum, the tiny slit glinting with promise. Javier maneuvered himself up onto an elbow then bent over and took a taste. Just one flick of his tongue and Malaki's flavor exploded across his taste buds. It had been so long since he'd tasted a man.

"You're delicious."

Mal dug his teeth into his lower lip and gripped the covers as if his life depended on it. Javier kissed the tight knuckles.

"You know, I really like how you keep your sac hairless but allow some tantalizing curls to highlight your impressive cock? Right now, I can see just how flushed your skin is, stretched taut in need of my touch."

He withdrew his fingers and applied a fresh coating of lube. Malaki's body sucked Javier in greedily as he pressed three fingers forward.

"I can't wait to feel this hot, tight ass clenching around my cock."

Mal's abs rippled as he drew in a deep breath. Javier finally gave in to his urge to trace the ink that decorated his lover's torso. He licked the intricate maze around Mal's pectoral, biting down with slow firm pressure around the peaked nipple.

"Javi… I'm…you're gonna make me come!"

"Not yet."

Mal's channel grasped Javier's fingers as he withdrew. Gloving up his cock took more concentration than ever before in his life. A good layer of slick and he knelt between Malaki's spread legs.

"You ready for this?"

"Fuck, yes. Take me hard."

If Mal wanted it hard, Javier had no trouble with that. He hoisted one of the tree limbs that acted as Malaki's legs onto his shoulder, twisting his body slightly to the side. Javier lined himself up and penetrated Mal's ass with all the authority of days past. The tight heat that surrounded his cock had him gasping and clutching Malaki as their curses and praises mingled together. He thrust deep, then paused. He opened his eyes to see a distinct flush beneath Mal's bronze skin.

The effort he put into the snap of his hips had sweat trickling down his back and the muscles throughout his body screaming with exertion. He loved this. Fucking a man fed his soul in a way that he could never eloquently put into words. Fucking Malaki was unlike any previous experience. He drove his cock deep, pegging his lover's gland with every thrust. Mal gasped and clawed at the sheets. He dug deep, too, for the willpower to hold back his own release, but the way Malaki was working his body in rhythm with Javier's made it more difficult with every second. Malaki's eyes flashed open and Javier was pulled into their hypnotic stare.

"Please."

He grasped Mal's dick and stroked with a grip that commanded without words. An anguished moan echoed throughout the room as though ripped from Malaki's soul. His seed spilled over Javier's hand in offering. His orgasm rushed through him and he came with a triumphant yell.

He carefully withdrew from Malaki's body and lowered his leg to the bed. He rolled to one side and collapsed, gasping to catch his breath.

"That was...you are...fuck me."

"We'll try that later. I think you wrung me dry."

"You know, that Fort Knox joke wasn't too far from the truth. Nobody's even touched my ass."

Malaki turned to face Javier. "Really? Not even a little?"

He shook his head. "But we'll figure it out together, right?"

Malaki cupped Javier's face and pulled him in for a kiss. "Right. Because I'm telling you right here and now...you are mine."

Malaki had claimed him and Javier's heart throbbed with happiness. It was a whole new world for him, but he was looking forward to exploring every twist and turn.

* * * *

"Five… Four… Three… Two… One!"

"Happy New Year!"

Malaki's ears rang with the cheers of fifty people. All around him, couples paired off for their first kiss of 2018. He looked around for Javier, but his lover had disappeared a while ago with Everett and Henry into the crowd filling the barn at the Brazos Walker Ranch. The party was the first of the kind he'd ever attended. Malaki typically celebrated the New Year quietly in his apartment in whatever city he'd landed in for the moment. The noise, the music, the crowd were one part overwhelming and one part contagious.

"If I'd known you were such a dancing queen, I'd have been showing you off in the clubs."

He would have spun around, but Javier locked his arms around his waist. He leaned back and moaned when Javier scraped his teeth on the back of his neck.

"I didn't know it myself. I've never had the desire to go deaf or get a blinding headache from swiveling lights until I had the opportunity to eye fuck you through a mass of gyrating bodies."

Javier came around and wrapped his arms around Malaki's neck. "Thank you. I know you, Brandon and Tyler basically planned this party for me."

He grasped Javier's hips and pulled him in closer. "I don't know what you could possibly be talking about."

Javier's eyes darkened and the lights cutting across the room highlighted the sharp angles of his cheekbones and jaw. His tawny beige skin glowed with a sheen of perspiration from dancing, and even through the sea of bodies engulfing them, Malaki was able to pick out his lover's unique scent.

"You know one of the things I love most about you?" Javier asked.

"What's that?"

"The fact that you always seem to know what I need even before I do. Just like this whole holiday season. I'm quite sure you don't typically build gingerbread houses, bake cookies, watch cheesy Christmas movies. And I know for damn sure that you've never played *Elf on the Shelf* before."

"Guilty. I had to Google that one, but hey, it was fun for the week. I think my favorite one was finding Edwin in the hot tub riding Ken."

Javier's laughter was more musical than the most popular song and his smile brighter than the moon reflecting off snow-covered peaks. Malaki pulled Javier out of the crowd and over to one of the semi-private corners.

"Look, all kidding aside. You've worked so hard to get your life back, but we haven't really taken the time to celebrate yet. We all thought this could be your new year of life, so to speak."

"I think that's one of the most sappily endearing and thoughtful things I've ever heard."

Javier fisted his shirt and tugged him till their chests collided. Malaki's pulse pounded as Javier gripped his neck and brought their mouths together. He pulled their bodies into a deeper, slower kiss, and hooked his arms around Javier's broad shoulders. Javier slid his hand down to grip Malaki's ass, his desire and hunger urging Mal's mouth open again. Blood pulsated through his veins and heart in a way that only Javier had ever incited.

"Let's take a walk."

They snuck outside and even Mal shivered with the blast of cold air compared to the warmth of the barn. An unusual winter front had invaded since Christmas, and he looked over at Javier, who didn't have as much muscle mass to generate heat. He wrapped his arm around his boyfriend and they meandered over towards one of the corrals. The horses were tucked away in their stables, no doubt under cozy blankets, knowing Tyler and way he spoiled those animals. Of course, if he had a cool million tied up in livestock, he'd probably treat them like babies too.

Javier took a long breath and sighed. "You know, the first time I came here, I'd never really been around horses before. But it didn't take me long to realize that these animals are special."

"I know. Today I kept looking at the stallions and thinking they're kings of their realm. There's just something that draws one's gaze, with their compelling presence."

Javier nudged his shoulder and pointed out in the field. The nearly full moon highlighted two bodies locked together in an embrace.

"Looks like we're not the only ones who had this idea."

"It's Brandon and Tyler. You know, when they first hooked up, I was a bit of a jack-off. I'd known both of them separately in the different phases of my life and, as selfish as it sounds, I was mad because it felt like the worlds that I'd worked so hard to put behind me were being shoved back in my face. But it wasn't long before I recognized how perfect they are for each other. Brandon has this hardness that Tyler softens without smoothing out the edges to take away his personality and Tyler needed someone who could accept his need to be a caregiver without expecting him to be a sugar daddy."

He'd seen exactly what Javier was describing over the last several days they'd spent on the ranch. Brandon often wore a deadpan expression worthy of a poker championship finals, until the moment Tyler appeared, often carrying the scents of sun, horses and hay. Then the mask would crack and Brandon glowed from the inside out. Malaki's people were not horsemen. He was a Pacific Islander to his soul. But even he could appreciate the rugged appeal of the man who'd spent countless hours and sweat molding this ranch and his horse breeding program into the success it had become. He looked down at Javier. Their gazes met and it felt as though their hearts collided, halting the progression of space and time.

Malaki wrapped his arms around Javier, ostensibly to keep him warm, but really just to hold on to this moment of perfection for a while longer. They kept their eyes on the couple out in the field. Even to a casual observer, it was evident their love was as expansive as the lush fields throughout the hill county where Tyler's ranch nestled.

"They came out here to be alone and here we are, spying on them."

Javier angled his head back and smiled. "Well, we could give them a run for their money?"

Malaki spun Javier around and lifted him up on to the top rail of the fence. "Wrap your legs around me."

He did tightly, making Malaki smile. Javier's position might be one of submission, but the man was letting it be said without words that Malaki didn't hold all the cards. Malaki unbuttoned Javier's shirt and the moment the cold air hit his chest, Javier hissed. His nipples beaded and Malaki sucked one into his mouth. Spanish curses whispered over his head. He gripped

Javier's back to hold him in place while the man arched into his possession.

He lifted his head and saw Tyler and Brandon standing just a few feet away, unabashedly watching them. He smiled as he kissed Javier's neck. He slid his hands up into Javier's hair and held the man exactly where he wanted him.

He placed his lips against Javier's ear and whispered, "We're being watched."

"Don't stop."

"Are you cold?"

"Never hotter."

He'd never been one for public displays, but this wasn't a display. It was a story. Javier the author and Malaki the narrator of a tale about a man who had traveled through the gates of hell and in doing so unlocked the truth of himself. Up until now, the words had only been shared between the two of them, but the time had come to release the work upon the world.

Their eyes met and it was as if Javier knew exactly what he was thinking, because he nodded, tightening his legs around Mal's waist. Malaki adjusted Javier so that he had more support on his precarious perch. Still clutching the strands of his hair, he pulled Javier's head back and slid his lips down the man's taut neck. He nipped Javier's Adam's apple. Javier's groan vibrated against his lips. He encircled Javier with his arms, surrounding the man with his love and passion. Their mouths met in a torrent of desire. He bit and licked at Javier's mouth, groaning when the man opened up and let him inside. He knew that they were supposed to be following a script. He needed to slow down, but the wet heat of Javier's mouth and the feel of his man's hands overrode all higher thought process.

Malaki heard footsteps and looked at Brandon and Tyler over Javier's shoulder. The men acted as though they were about to leave, but he met Brandon's gaze and gave a slight shake of his head.

He wants you to see this. Listen to what he's saying.

Tyler nodded and held Brandon close. Malaki pulled at Javier's shirt, still tucked into his jeans, until he touched the hot, hard flesh of Javier's slim waist with the tips of his fingers. The skin was tight and hot. He gripped the back of Javier's shirt and ripped the covering away.

Malaki slid his hand over the curve of Javier's backbone and pulled him in, tucking the man's head against his shoulder. Soft panting breaths against his skin and Javier's grip against his shoulders gave away the nerves strumming through his lover. The moonlight exposed crisscrossing scars from each lash of the whip and sear of the brand. Twin gasps cut across the field, sharper than the wind that blasted down from the Artic, threatening to freeze everything around them. But in his arms, Javier was warm and alive.

He stroked his hand down Javier's back, feeling the shiver of awareness slide down Javier's spine. He knew without asking that the reaction was a potent mixture of desire and acceptance. Malaki found Javier's gaze again. His people had believed that humans' courses in history had been set when the moon gave birth to the stars. He wasn't so sure about absolute destiny, but something in the universe had led the four of them to this spot. Under the naked light of the moon, Javier revealed to the world the man he'd become.

Chapter Eleven

Javier took a look around his apartment. Outside, the freshly planted trees of the complex were sprouting the first green leaves of the spring. The new construction was a nice upgrade from the rundown assisted housing he'd been staying in, but not as flashy as his old place. Overall, it fit the revived him pretty well. The complex was equally distant to his work and Mal's place, so that was a bonus too. The eight-hundred-and-fifty-square-foot space actually felt cavernous compared to his cell and the studio he'd been staying in since his return to Dallas.

"Where do you want me to put this dining room table?" Malaki asked as he walked in through the front door.

"How about the dining area?"

"Okay, smart ass. Where have you designated your dining area to be?"

His apartment had a combination living-dining room. There was an extended countertop that divided the kitchen from the living room, but Javier still wanted some kind of table where he could sit down.

"I was thinking over by the door to the balcony."

The delivery people had brought in the big pieces from the rental place yesterday, but Javier had wanted to buy one piece of new furniture that was his alone. It just happened to have worked out that he was dating a man with a big truck to get it home.

"I still think this was a futastic idea of Brandon's."

The muscles bunched in Mal's shoulders and arms as he carried the furniture across the room. The round table was made of wood and iron. Not exactly light, but his man made it seem as though it was as easy as the plastic set he'd used in his college apartment.

"Javi? Hello!"

"Sorry, what?

Mal smiled and posed against the glass wall leading to his balcony. "Were you staring at my ass?"

"Nope."

Javier couldn't help but laugh at the hang-dog expression on his lover's face. It was such fun to tease the big man. "Your bulging biceps may have caught my attention, though." Malaki flexed and Javier rolled his eyes. "Please. There's no need to troll for compliments."

Mal's eyes darkened and Javier found himself backing up until he hit the breakfast bar. He could have escaped when Malaki's arms imprisoned him against the granite, but they both knew he wanted to be there.

"So you didn't hear what I said earlier?"

"When?"

"As I labored arduously to get your furniture in place?"

"Uh-uh."

"I said I still think this was a futastic idea of Brandon's. I—"

"A fu-what?"

"Futastic. Fucking fantastic. See, I combined the two words, like Bennifer. It works. No?"

Javier shook his head. "No. Not to mention it kinda shows your age, since they haven't been together since like decades ago."

"Well, the classics never die. Now, as I was saying before you so rudely interrupted me… I never would have thought about using a house staging company to lease furniture from. Filling a house is expensive and this way you get to save up to buy one quality piece at a time instead of filling your new place with cheap fake wood furniture from discount stores."

"Mm-hm. He has lots of moments of brilliance. We're just careful about letting him know it. Speaking of my new furniture, how about we break in that new bed of mine?"

"We could." Malaki leaned down and buried his face in Javier's neck. "Or I could fuck you right here against the counter."

His breath caught and his muscles tightened. They'd breached a lot of the walls in Javier's mind that had sealed him off from experiencing the connection two people shared together. But this was the first time Malaki had brought up plans to storm the fortress. Javier truly didn't know where his reluctance came from. Each time he and Malaki were together blew his mind. Javier slid his hands up Malaki's chest and massaged his shoulders. The big man moaned and turned to jelly under Javier's skilled hands.

"We could." He kissed the jugular notch at the base of Mal's throat. "Or I can strip you down and massage your entire body as a thank you for helping me move. You know how good I am. I bet I can turn you into a pile of goo. Really reach the deepest…muscles to give you the greatest pleasure."

Malaki grabbed Javier's hand and had started to drag him to the bedroom when there was a knock on the door. If looks could have killed, whoever stood behind that door would have been vaporized.

"Sorry. Guess you'll have to take a rain check." He pulled Malaki down and sealed their lips together. Javier's awareness of the world narrowed to the existence of Malaki's touch. Their connection consumed him in a way that would have been terrifying had he not trusted Mal with the security of his soul.

The door rattled with the force of another knock. "Come on, guys. Get your clothes on—this stuff is heavy!"

Malaki snickered and Javier rolled his eyes. *Leave it to Brandon to be ever so tactful.* Javier sauntered over to the door and opened it with a deliberate slowness.

"Finally!"

"Serves you right for being such a drama queen," Tyler said as he entered behind his partner.

Brandon set down the bag of stuff from the home store they'd raided earlier that day. "I am not a drama queen."

"Normally I would agree with you, but when the mood hits, you can rival the greatest Cher had to offer."

"Well, at least that means I look amazing in leather. Now, where would you like us to put all this stuff?"

"Counter is fine for now. I'll sort and figure out where to put everything later."

Javier had tried to rein in the shopping frenzy, wanting to keep his clutter to only the basics. Initially he'd told Brandon he planned on shopping for kitchen stuff at the dollar store and the man had nearly had an aneurysm. They'd reached a compromise, but even with only buying the essentials Javier had nearly had a heart attack at the register. And while the balance in his bank account might be significantly less, he regretted nothing. His life had revolved around imprisonment, torture and recovery for so long. Ultimately, he'd found his way back to life and learned how to love for the first time. He deserved a few treats.

"You look a little far away. Everything all right?" Malaki asked softly as he wrapped his arms around Javier from behind.

He leaned back and accepted Malaki's support. Accepting someone else's strength was still new, but each time he grew to appreciate the offer a little more.

"Right now, I'm the luckiest person in the world. You know I talk a big game, but there were days when I was moments away from breaking. Where seconds stretched into eons of hell, and my heart shattered from the explosions of hate."

He turned in Mal's arms and looked up at him. He cupped Malaki's cheek and stared into his eyes. Everyone wore masks to survive in today's world, but Mal's mask was off and Javier saw the rawness of his soul. Everything was exposed and Javier shook with the enormity of the offering. It was his to accept or reject. If he accepted, then there was no going back. Their lives would be united forever on a molecular level. If he rejected, then Malaki would survive, but his heart would carry scars deeper than the ones that marred Javier's body.

"I survived, but I'm alive become of you. You healed my heart and allowed me to find my soul. I love you, Malaki Taupo."

Malaki's eyes glistened. He swallowed a couple of times, as though the words that were desperate to break free were barricaded.

"Until I met you, I was a nomad. My life was full but my spirit empty, triggering a restlessness that kept me moving. I didn't even know what I was searching for until you walked into my life, full of resolve and a soul carved by experience beyond your years. You faced the devil, but didn't allow his fires to consume you. The moment our eyes met, I knew I'd found my home. You *are* my heart, Javier."

Their foreheads touched and Javier inhaled Malaki's breaths. He absorbed the words of love and let them fill the cavities within him till happiness emanated from his pores.

"Seeing you smile is what I live for each day."

"That's a large expectation to live up to. What if I'm having the world's shittiest day?"

"Then, on those days, it'll be my job to help you find it again. That's what being a partner is about."

"Well, that and making sure the people who help him move get free drinks, because God knows Javier doesn't have enough social tact to remember."

Javier looked over at Brandon, who stood there grinning from ear to ear. "You carried two bags up from the car, most of which you made me buy in the first place."

He scoffed. "Please. If I'd left you to your own devices, you'd be eating off paper plates and with plastic utensils."

Tyler put his arm around Brandon and placed his lips next to his ear. "At least Javier knows how to cook food to put on his plates."

"Hey, I'm getting better!"

"Yes, love. You managed to successfully craft an excellent turkey and cheese sandwich the other day."

"I'm sorry, weren't you the one who said the toasted bread made all the difference?"

"Guys! I swear I think the two of you use bickering as a form of foreplay."

Tyler winked and Malaki chuckled behind Javier. Brandon walked over and gave Javier a hug.

"It's a nice place, and I'm really happy for you," he whispered.

Clearly his friends had overheard his and Mal's confessions a few moments ago.

"Thanks. Do you want to stay and eat dinner off my new plates? I have nothing edible here, but I did manage to bring the amaretto sour mixers from my old place."

"Now that's a man who's thinking! Forget the food and bring on the booze."

Tyler cleared his throat and Brandon sighed.

"Thank you, but we can't. I have to actually be a grown-up. There are covers due tomorrow and you know Tyler can't go more than a few hours without talking to his babies."

He gave Brandon a hug. "Have a safe drive and text when you guys get home."

"Yes, Mom."

Javier saw them out of the door after receiving a hug from Tyler. Then it was just him and Mal. He turned and met his lover's gaze. "Now, how about that massage?"

Chapter Twelve

"Today is my alive day."

Malaki grasped the bowl of popcorn, two beers and the movie he'd picked up from Redbox. Javier had said he wanted a quiet night at home when they'd texted at lunchtime.

"What's that?"

"It's a thing that I've heard some of the people in my trauma support group talk about. Mainly vets. For one guy, he celebrates the day his got his leg blown off by an IED but he lived."

Mal stopped walking and did a quick mental assessment of the calendar. "Today's the anniversary of the day you escaped."

Javier nodded. "One year ago, my life started over. I thought about celebrating in October, on the day he took me, but that didn't feel right."

Mal set the stuff down on the coffee table and sat on the sofa. He took Javier's hand.

"Why not?"

"Well, that day was really the start of the darkest part of my life and the whole point of alive day is to celebrate the day you stared death in the eye and came out the other side. So today seemed much more appropriate."

"If it's something we're celebrating, why don't we get dressed and go out for a nice dinner?"

"Really?"

"Sure. Why not?" He stood and held out his hand. "Come on, sexy. Let's go."

Javier smiled and stood. Malaki led them into his bedroom. They'd started keeping a few changes of clothes at each other's places. It wasn't long before they'd both shed their comfy after-work clothes and slid into suits.

Malaki secured his watch and looked over at Javier. It had required months of hard work, but the man was finally back up to a decent fighting weight. Malaki had taken great pleasure in constructing nutrition and workout plans to maximize Javier building muscle mass again. His knee was as strong as possible after reconstruction. His mind was in a good place since he continued to work sporadically with a therapist, and Malaki had the health of his heart well in hand. Had he known about alive day, he would have made the occasion much more significant.

"You ready?" Javier asked

"Always. Where do you want to go?"

"I don't really know. It's not like I dine in upscale restaurants on a regular basis."

"Me, neither." He snapped his fingers. "Let's call in a solid."

Javier smiled and whipped out his phone. "Hey, Tyler, I have a question. If we wanted to hit up a really nice place to have a celebration dinner without having made advance reservations, where would we go?"

"Well, my family traditionally goes to The Mansion for special nights out, but it's impossible to get in without a reservation. Unless…."

"Unless what?"

"Leave it to me. Head to Turtle Creek Boulevard. The restaurant is located in the old Rosewood mansion. Now, since I'm about to call in a favor of my own, what exactly are you celebrating?"

"My alive day."

"Consider it done. Have a nice night, guys."

Javier disconnected the call and scooped up his keys. "I'm driving!"

They jumped into Javier's car. Well, he jumped and Malaki squeezed. He'd purchased a used coupe once he'd trusted himself to be fit enough to drive again. But his shopping considerations had not included a towering boyfriend with hulking muscles. Mal slid the seat all the way back and wedged his body into the car. Javier heard a soft grunt and clearly hadn't rid himself of all his assholishness, because a tiny grin escaped when he glanced over and saw how ridiculous Mal looked.

"Do you want to take your truck?"

"No, you called dibs fair and square."

Javier held out his hand. "I said I was driving. Not that we had to take my car."

"Thank fucking God!"

Malaki tossed him the keys and miraculously exited the vehicle ten times faster than he'd gotten in. Javier locked up his car. He patted the roof. "It's not your fault."

"Stop making out with your car and let's go. I'm hungry."

"I don't know how a man who eats so much is constantly hungry."

"I didn't hear you complaining the other night when I had your cock shoved down my throat."

He climbed into the driver's seat of Malaki's truck. "Hmm, maybe tonight I'll let you have my ass for dessert."

Javier got everything adjusted for a normal-sized person and started the engine. He looked over at Mal to see how the man had responded to his little bomb.

"I'm trying really hard to play it cool right now."

He took Mal's hand. "I'm not fucking with you. I think I'm ready. At least for some stuff and we'll see how it goes." He turned to face his lover and kissed his hand. "You know it's never been a matter of not wanting you, right? My body craves every touch and kiss. I've even—" He cleared his throat. "I've even played with my ass in the shower a few times. I figured if I can get used to a sexual touch from my own fingers, it wouldn't feel so foreign when you do it."

Malaki visibly relaxed and cupped Javier's cheek. "It's always been at your pace. You know that. Now, having said that, I feel obligated to tell you that I am so fucking turned on right now at the thought of you fingering yourself. Did it feel good?"

Javier nodded.

"Did you come?"

"Almost. Can we skip dinner?" he whispered

Malaki sat back in the seat and smiled. "Nope. We're going out, and the both of us are going suffer to the point that by the time we get home these fancy clothes will be in real danger of being destroyed. Now, to The Mansion, Jeeves."

"Thanks for the blue balls, you bastard," Javier mumbled

Malaki took Javier's hand and put it over his crotch. The stiff cock beneath his slacks filled his hand and Javier moaned.

"Just think about how glorious you're going to feel when you shoot your wad all over my ink in a couple of hours."

"God damn it, Mal!" he shouted as he ripped his hand away and gripped the steering wheel hard.

Malaki's deep chuckle filled the cab and Javier adjusted himself. The traffic on the 75 was worse than he would have expected this time of night, requiring a modicum of concentration to keep them from getting tangled up and missing the exit. Thank God for the GPS whose pleasant British voice told them they'd arrived at their destination twenty-five minutes later.

Imposing oak trees lined the cobblestoned driveway as they pulled up to the mansion that had been converted to an exclusive restaurant and boutique hotel. The valet stood beside an awning, but there was no obvious parking lot.

"I guess we're about to find out how the other half lives."

"This place is amazing."

If he was being honest, he was a little intimidated by the imposing luxury spread out in front of them. He glanced at Mal out of the corner of his eye to see if he was alone. Mal was peering through the windshield, like a child's face pressed up against the glass of a toy store.

"We are going to look like a couple of gawking tourists."

Mal took Javier's hand as they pulled up to the valet station. "No way. We're going to own this joint."

He was right. There was a time Javier wouldn't have thought anything about making reservations here and treating a date to a special night out, and it was time to take back that last bit of his old life.

The valet opened his door. "Evening, sir."

Javier got out, holding his head up high. He handed over the keys to Malaki's truck. "Hello. Thank you very much."

The valet looked a bit shocked then smiled. Javier guessed he didn't hear those words often. *Well, there's no reason not to treat someone with respect.* He walked around the front of the truck and joined Malaki. His insides warmed as Mal rested his hand on Javier's lower back and guided him inside. The subtle statement let everyone know that they were together and not ashamed to show it.

"May I help you, gentlemen?"

"I believe there should be a reservation for Alde?"

The hostess took her sweet time examining the tablet, while peeking up at Malaki through her eyelashes. The light blue dress shirt and navy suit stood out against his skin and the soft lights did nothing to minimize the power of his body.

Mal filled the entry hall both physically and with a presence that people just couldn't avoid, as was evident by several stares from other diners and staff. Just then Mal turned and looked down at Javier. He'd never stood a chance from the moment Mal's gleaming smile and dark eyes focused on him. The hostess let out the tiniest bit of a sigh.

Yes, he's a fucking stud and he's all mine.

"*Love you,*" he mouthed.

"Right this way. Is this your first time with us?"

"Yes. Your establishment was recommended by a friend," Malaki answered.

"I saw that notation on the reservation. We pride ourselves not only on the cuisine but also the experience. As you can see, the mansion has a distinct European decor with ornate details. You gentlemen will be dining in what was once the owner's private study. It's one of our more intimate rooms."

They entered the room and Javier had to keep himself from freezing on the spot. His gaze bounced from the dark wood paneling that covered the walls to a massive carved fireplace, across the arched ceiling with the plaster reliefs and down the leaded windows.

"Here you are."

The hostess had led them to a table right by the fireplace. It might have been spring, but the fireplace was lit, throwing a warm glow across the room. He sank into the plush high-backed chair and met Mal's gaze across the table.

"So, what do you think?"

"I think Tyler has a lot more strings to pull than I ever gave him credit for."

Javier nodded. "Tyler likes to play the small-time ranch owner and breeder, but his name is known across the country. On top of that, his family is like Dallas royalty. It might have been his dream to ride his horses across the hills and not a desk in the corporate office, but never doubt he has the kind of power only a few can lay claim to."

He was so caught up in looking at all the features in the room that Javier jumped when their waiter appeared out of nowhere.

"Gentlemen, my name is Evan and I will be your server. I understand that you're celebrating a special occasion tonight. I've been informed that a private party spoke with our chef and they arranged your meal and drink selections. Are you amenable to their selections?"

Mal did his one-eyebrow trick and Javier smiled. "I'm game. How about you?"

"I believe that we should live this experience to the fullest."

"Very well." Evan brought out a bottle of wine and presented the label. "To start, I have a bottle of cabernet blend from Destree Vineyards. You'll notice notes of violets, raspberries and dried herbs. It's very smooth and has just a touch of vanilla in the after-taste."

Javier nodded and the server went about presenting the glasses with a quiet competency that, despite Javier's lack of knowledge when it came to wines, didn't make him feel awkward.

Malaki raised his glass. "To celebrating life. I'm honored you've chosen to share yours with me."

He swallowed and refused to acknowledge the fact that his vision wavered slightly with emotion. He lifted his glass and gently touched it to Malaki's. "I..." He cleared his throat. "We never know where the diversions of our paths in life may lead, but I am so glad mine led to you."

Malaki's eyes burned with an intensity that Javier had only seen in the quiet moments of intimacy they shared. They stared at each other as they sipped the wine. The flickering comfort from the fireplace was nothing compared to the all-consuming warmth he found in Malaki's presence. Tonight truly was a celebration of not only his survival, but their life moving forward together.

* * * *

"Are you sure about this?"

Javier slid his hands up Malaki's bare chest and around his neck. The pounding of Malaki's pulse matched Javier's. "More than. I want to share everything I am with you."

"I believe you, but that doesn't have to mean *everything*. I know you love me. You don't have to prove anything to me."

Javier shook his head. "That's not what this is about. For years I purposefully held part of myself away from my lovers, both physically and emotionally. Being with you has taught me that the emotional walls prevented me from experiencing the very connection I've been desperately seeking. I trust you to help me break through the last of the physical walls I built around myself. Maybe it sounds stupid, but I think if I never try, then I'm still holding something back. And that's not what I want for us. I fought to escape that hell. I fought to get my life back. And I want to fight for us."

Malaki took Javier in his arms. "I know you do. But loving each other is not about fighting. It's about sharing. Sharing our lives and, yes, sharing our bodies, but only in ways that fulfill us."

"That's funny, because I thought that's what I was asking for you to do."

"What?"

"Fill me up. Fill me with everything you have till my heart and body are bursting and I have no choice but to release the last ounce of darkness inside me. Because from tonight forward, I want there to only be room for light."

He pulled Malaki to him and pressed their lips together, lingering till his flesh tingled and his head spun. Javier closed his eyes, and with each second that passed he realized this connection he shared with Mal was the most vital thing in his life.

Javier pressed his face against Malaki's thickly muscled chest. Layers of scents enveloped Mal's body. The clean-smelling soap that still clung mixed with his cologne that, although evaporated, still exuded a musky fragrance. Javier traced the shapes of Mal's tattoo over the broad expanse of his pectoral. By the time he reached the jutting tip of his textured nipple, Malaki was breathing fast. Mal held Javier's face against him with his large hands. Whispering pleas reached his ears and Javier had no trouble complying. There was nothing better than making Malaki writhe in pleasure. He circled the nub with his tongue and bit the puckering skin, cheering on the inside when Mal gasped and jammed his hips forward.

Javier didn't let up. He abused one nipple with his teeth and flicked the other with his fingernail. Malaki's body was so taut that Javier skipped his fingers across the ridges of muscles standing out against his torso and stomach. He wrapped his hands around Mal's hard cock, fisting it tight. The slick fluid leaking from the tip eased the friction as he did his best to bring out Mal's sexy growl.

"God, I can't decide if you're an angel or the devil." He clutched Javier's wrists and held them tight. "But either way, you can't tempt me away from that glorious ass of yours." He herded Javier toward the bed.

Javier found himself flying backward onto the bed. The mattress cradled him in a cloud of softness as Malaki came down over him. "Did you just throw me?"

"Yes. Now, where did we stash the lube?"

He stretched his arms over his head, elongating his body. Mal's gaze darkened with appreciation. Suddenly he found himself a victim of Malaki's mouth and fingers. Mal played Javier's body with the expertise of a virtuoso. The haze of lust cleared enough for Javier to realize that Mal had been holding back. Till now he'd been feeding Javier nibbles off the Malaki Taupo sexual buffet. His body vibrated with tension that he would normally have unleashed upon his lover to make his body explode with pleasure. But right then, Mal refused to let Javier capture even a single breath, and he found he rather enjoyed it. He brushed against the lube on the bedside table and, with an effort born of desperation, gripped the tube and tossed it across the space between them. Malaki must have had eyes on the side of his head because, faster than a cobra strike, the man snatched it out of the air.

"Get me ready?"

Javier lifted his legs, and if they trembled a little, he was going to chalk it up to an errant muscle spasm, but before he could work up another response to the question that appeared in Malaki's eyes, Mal took him in a ferocious, wet kiss, sweeping the inside of Javier's mouth from back to front with his masterful tongue. *Is that me whimpering?* He threw his arms around Mal's neck, arching his body into the heat of Malaki's chest and the hard line of his questing mouth. A growl of approval vibrated all the way down to his ankles that gripped Malaki's narrow hips.

"Don't make me wait any more, please?"

Mal ground his cock against the crease of Javier's ass, and he blinked up at Mal.

"You think you're ready?"

He nodded, but his eyes went wide when Malaki popped the top of the lube. The click suddenly took on a whole new meaning from this position. Mal's usually glittering eyes darkened as he squeezed out a generous amount of the clear liquid. Javier unwound his legs and folded them up until his feet were flat against Malaki's chest.

"All those hours of yoga have paid off, huh?"

"Want to see just how flexible I've gotten?"

"You do that, and the slow sweet seduction is going out the window and you're going to get fucked to within an inch of your life."

Javier's cock jumped against his stomach. "That's exactly what I want."

Any further words flew out of his brain as Mal pushed Javier's knees up over his shoulders, exposing his ass to Malaki's slippery fingers. The foreign touch made him squirm until those digits touched his puckered hole with intentional pressure. Javier's sphincter contracted, partly in anticipation and partly in trepidation. Then the experiment became reality as Mal slid one of his fingers inside Javier's ass and worked his tight hole.

"Oh, fuck…"

"Is that a good fuck or a bad fuck?"

Javier smiled through the foreign sensations racketing through his body. "Is there such a thing as a bad fuck?"

"Not if I'm doing this right."

"You're… Oh, God, there… You're doing it right."

Mal gave him another finger, and Javier sucked in a breath before forcing his muscles to relax and accept the stretch. Mal twisted his wrist, sliding his fingers deeper into Javier's body, using his thumb to stroke the ring of muscle. He appreciated Mal's concern for his uninitiated ass, but it was going to take more than two fingers to prepare him for the cock he'd become intimately familiar with in every other way.

"Give me more. Don't hold anything back from me."

"Never. Everything I have is yours."

Mal added a third finger and something unlocked within Javier. It was as if the deepest cell inside him that craved this moment multiplied exponentially and every nerve ending came alive, begging for Mal to become their control center.

"Ready?"

"Take me."

Malaki slid his fingers away, but before Javier could evaluate how he'd changed on a fundamental level, Mal guided his gloved cock to his entrance. Javier held his breath. His heart and head swelled with so much emotion as Mal pushed the crown of his cock inside that he stared up at his lover through wavering vision.

"Oh, Javi, I've got you."

The thickness of Malaki's shaft stretched his tender channel. Javier tried to take deep breaths and for the first time understood how pain and pleasure could co-exist in a way that a man's understanding of the world transformed. Malaki peppered Javier with kisses as he pulled and pushed, breaking through psychological as well as physical barriers until he was finally buried deep inside.

"That's it. You did it, Javi. I'm all the way inside you."
He's inside me.

In ways that Javier didn't even have the words to explain right then. Mal rocked gently inside Javier, just barely moving. It was the sweetest, scariest sensation Javier had ever known. He couldn't look away as words of thanks and love were locked deep inside him. Malaki's face contorted with pleasure each time his cock stroked in and out of Javier's body. And while Mal could have given into the demands of his body, his eyes swore that he hadn't forgotten his pledge.

"Are you okay?" Mal said between panted breaths.

"I…I feel like I don't know myself. My body is on fire for more, and all I want to do is make you my anchor in this storm swarming in my mind."

"Your mind has given you shelter in so many storms throughout your life, but right now I'm your shelter. I'll protect both your body and your mind."

Javier cupped Mal's cheek. His brow glistened as his body worked to reshape Javier's understanding of pleasure. "I know."

Malaki suddenly shifted Javier's legs back around his waist again and planted his hands over Javier's shoulders. Now that he wasn't pinned, Javier started moving with each of Mal's thrusts, lifting and sliding his channel against Malaki's cock. Regaining some control unleashed a hunger inside him. He gripped Malaki's shoulders and it almost seemed as if his ink came alive, unleashing a power within him to send Javier soaring into a space where his body and mind lived on another plane of existence.

Mal gritted his teeth, shifting his weight. The sharp features of his face blurred and Javier pushed out a guttural moan.

"It's about to get real, Javi."

Before he could respond, Malaki plastered a hard, searing kiss against his lips. Jerking his hips back, he took everything away from Javier until just the tip of his cock sat inside the tight ring of his hole, then he shifted downward, plunging back in, and sent Javier's channel into a frenzy of sensation. It felt so damned good to be taken in such a way, so completely, because he knew it was Mal. The man he loved. The man who fostered such a desperate need in Javier that he ached to give Malaki everything he was.

Javier dug his fingers into the muscles of Mal's back as his lover jammed his erection in deep once more, grinding Javier against the mattress. There would be bruises on his thighs in the morning, but Javier would wear the marks with pride. Malaki's thrusts set Javier's insides on fire to the point that he feared he'd spontaneously combust if there wasn't some kind of release soon. Javier cried out, his ass spasming in unparalleled delight as Malaki fucked him.

"Soon, Javi."

"Do it. I'm so close. I can't believe you're about to make me come like this. I haven't even touched my dick."

Malaki slid a hand beneath Javier's neck and lifted his head, colliding their lips in a carnal kiss unlike any he'd experienced before. He groaned, and Mal did too, both dueling for dominance that neither were willing to give up anytime soon. Malaki's thrusts started to get less purposeful and more erratic. Javier loved it. Loved how even in this position he had the power to make his lover lose control. He clenched the muscles in his ass as tightly as he could, knowing that in his experience the vise-like grip often sent him tumbling over the edge of oblivion.

"Give it to me, Mal. I want to feel your cum shoot from your cock like a geyser."

"Oh, fucking Christ!"

Malaki shuddered and moaned above him. Their gazes found each other and locked. Mal's skin drew taut over his sharp cheekbones and his lips pulled back to expose bright teeth.

"I'm coming."

Malaki shoved his cock deep inside Javier's ass, filling him deeper than ever before. Javier couldn't hold back his moan, but any discomfort no longer mattered as above him, Mal threw his head back, his seed flooding the condom as he came. Javier wrapped his arms around Mal and held on, his breaths gasping from his chest and the valve inside him finally released, and as tears of joy spilled from his eyes, he gave a great cry of completion.

Chapter Thirteen

Malaki clicked open an email and frowned. The screen went a little blurry and his ears rang.

"What the hell?"

He let out a slow breath as nausea rolled through him like a freight train.

"You okay, boss man?" Bethany asked.

"Umm, not really. Is my next patient here yet?"

"Nope. You don't look so good."

Mal jumped up and ran for the bathroom. He promptly lost every ounce of the protein shake, strawberries, and almonds he'd just finished for breakfast. As soon as he stood, the room spun and he grabbed the wall. Another wave of nausea swamped him and down he went. This time there was just bile and dry heaving. Just then his stomach gurgled and he had to do some quick maneuvering before he had a serious problem to contend with.

"Oh, fuck."

Several minutes later he made his way back toward his office. As soon as he sat down at his desk, it felt like

Niagara Falls was pouring from his forehead. He popped a mint from his drawer into his mouth and laid his forehead on his desk.

Bethany handed Malaki a cool cloth. "Carrie had a cancelation and took your patient. I've already started calling the rest of your schedule. You are going home."

"I can't. I have so much to do today."

"Malaki, you have sick days for a reason."

"But the patients are counting on me too—" He grabbed his trash can and dry heaved several more times.

"Counting on you to transmit the plague to them? Go. Home."

He nodded as he continued to lean over the can. "Just let me get the room to stop spinning first."

"Do you want me to call Javier? I don't think you should be driving."

"I'll be fine. I just need a few minutes. I don't know where this came from. I was perfectly fine when I woke up this morning. Didn't feel anything off with Mr. Bader."

"Well, that's what happens with stomach flu. It can happen really fast."

He used the cloth to wipe his still dripping forehead. "Yeah. Thank you for everything. And please tell the rest of the patients that I'm really sorry."

"I'm sure they understand. It happens to all of us."

Malaki worked to get a few more things cleared off his desk while trying to evaluate if it was safe to leave. It took him twice as long to get home since he had to stop three times and find a bathroom. As soon as he pulled into the parking lot of his condo, he let out a breath.

"Thank fucking God."

He trudged up the steps to his front door. As soon as he got inside, he pulled out his phone and clicked on his text icon for Javier.

Went home sick. Stay away for your own safety.

He changed out of his work clothes and put on some ratty old sweats and a T-shirt. He heard Javier's ringtone go off in the living room.

"What's wrong? You're never sick!"

"Stomach virus or something. Just started throwing up at work."

"You're not pregnant, are you?"

"Very funny, asshole."

"Sorry, is there anything I can do?"

"No, I just wanted to warn you away so you don't catch whatever hell has befallen me. How's your day going so far? What did we eat last night?"

"Umm, grilled salmon with that sweet and spice rub."

"Oh yeah. That was good. You're feeling okay, though."

"Yeah, babe. I'm fine. Look, I left some sparkling water there. Get a glass, relax on the sofa, put on a movie and do not remote into the office. I'll call and check on you at lunch time."

"Mmkay." He curled up on his bed. "I might take a nap. I feel like I got hit in the gut by a hundred and four mile an hour fastball."

"Now I know you're really sick. You never nap."

He closed his eyes and started to drift off.

"Love you, Mal."

"Love you, too," he said, already drifting off.

* * * *

Malaki blinked and groaned as the light filtering through his bedroom window shot through his eyeballs, triggering a massive headache. "Fuck me."

His body ached as though he'd gone thirty rounds in an octagon, and his clothes felt as if he'd walked twenty miles through a swamp. It seemed the only thing that didn't hurt was his ears, and they picked up sounds coming from outside his bedroom. "What the hell?"

Well, if someone's here to murder me, at least they'll put me out of my misery.

His bedroom door was pushed open and in walked Javier, carrying a tray.

"Hey, I brought you some toast and bubbles. How are you feeling?"

"I thought I told you to stay away."

"You did. I ignored you."

Malaki scooted up so he could prop his back against the headboard. Javier set the tray across his lap and he couldn't decide if the offering was the best thing he'd ever seen or the antichrist.

Javier whipped out a laminated card with a bunch of printed faces on it. "Now, on a scale of happy face to tears how bad is your pain? Oh no, judging by that face, we've reached Defcon level two of the grumpiness scale."

"Two? What's level one?"

"One is when you're throwing dishes at my head and telling me to get the fuck out."

He sighed. As bad as he felt, he didn't want to be the guy who took it out on the people around him. He picked up the card and the dry erase pen Javier held out to him then drew a skull and crossbones.

"Hmm, I see. Well, I have just the thing to make you feel better."

Javier leaned over and kissed Malaki on the forehead. Amazingly enough, he did feel incrementally better. He reached out and took Javi's hand. "Stay?"

"Always. Try to have a little snack. I'm going to change and then we can cuddle in to watch a movie or something."

Javier stripped his shirt off and shucked his cargos that he'd worn to work. Mal might have felt like death, but clearly the end wasn't upon him yet, because he couldn't look away from his lover's body as he walked across the room and rummaged through the drawer where he kept a few changes of clothes. Normally he never focused on Javier's scars, but, for some reason, today they stood out like neon signs. Instantly, he felt so much worse for being such a baby about a little flu bug.

"Thank you for bringing me the snack and everything, but I really need a shower and to get out of this bed."

"Okay. Need any help? Have you taken anything lately?"

He shook his head. "You know NSAIDs wreck your gut and I've had enough problems with that today. But you'd be a lifesaver if you'd brew me a cup of willow bark tea and get some hot and cold compresses ready."

"Done." Javier helped Mal out of bed and made sure he was steady on his feet. "Are you sure you don't need to go to urgent care or something?"

He took Javier in his arms. "I'm sure. Just a little virus bug. Gotta let it run its course."

"Okay, but if your head starts spinning in circles and you talk in tongues, we are reevaluating the situation."

"Fair enough. Now back away before I get you sick."

"Hey, you pulled me in!"

"I know. I just couldn't help myself."

Javier pulled Malaki down and rubbed their noses together. "You don't know how glad I am to hear that. And for the record, being here to make sure you're taken care of is worth the risk."

Jesus, he didn't know what magical penny he found to land a man like Javier, but as sucky as today had been, he was glad that life had shown him a way to remind him of that.

Malaki felt marginally better after his shower and getting into some clean clothes. He stepped outside his bedroom and detected the scent of the tea drifting from the kitchen. He peered into the pass-through and saw Javier doing a little salsa dance to some song playing from his phone. Javi never expressed his heritage outwardly very often. Despite him being fluent in Spanish, Malaki had never really heard him say more than a phrase or two occasionally. Or if he was feeling particularly sentimental sometimes, the tones of Spanish guitar music could be heard flowing through his apartment.

"Why is that?"

Javier spun around and gasped. "Holy shit, you scared me."

That was saying something, because when they'd first met, Javier had seemed almost hypervigilant of his surroundings. Much like Malaki had seen with service members when he'd worked in San Diego.

"Sorry. I was having a conversation in my head. Now I'll include you."

"Okay?"

"I was just wondering why you don't let out your heritage more often. I mean, I know you're half Mexican."

Javier carried over the mug of tea. "I don't purposely hide it. I speak Spanish when needed, and if someone asks, I tell them about *mi familia*. Or at least the basics of where I come from."

"You know if you ever want to talk about what really happened with your family, you can."

Javier came around the post to stand next to Malaki. "I know. I guess I just figured each person is only allowed one sob story per lifetime. I moved on from their abandonment a long time ago, and besides, they're all dead or gone now so it's not like some magical reunion is possible."

"Wait, what?"

"*Si, mis abuelos* died not long after I finished college and I was notified that my mother went back to Mexico after their deaths. She still had family there. I never saw my father again after he left, so I have no idea where he is or what happened to him."

"So your mother is Mexican and your father is American?"

"Partly right. My mother was born and raised in Guadalajara. When my grandparents came to the US on a work visa in the mid-nineties, she was sixteen. She was introduced to my father, who was Puerto Rican and worked for the same manufacturing engineering company as my grandfather. They were married just after she turned eighteen and I arrived a year later."

"Don't take this the wrong way, but did she marry your father for a green card?"

Javier shook his head. "I was told that part of the arrangement was my father wouldn't marry her until she was naturalized."

"So…your mother held dual citizenship, but chose to return to Mexico?"

Javier shrugged. "There was nothing to keep her here."

"You?"

He shook his head. "Shortly before I finished my bachelors, I came out, and them being proper pious Catholics, they all disavowed me."

Malaki took Javier into his arms. It certainly hadn't been his intention to start a conversation that went down this path. For being an event that probably had destroyed his world at the time, Javier spoke about it very matter-of-factly. He might feel it qualified as a sob story, but Malaki just saw it as another layer that made up the man he loved.

"You know, you never really talk about your family much, either. I mean, you talk *to* them all the time, but not really about them."

"Huh. Yeah, I guess you're right."

"So glad to feel validated."

"Smartass." He took Javier's hand and led him over to the sofa. Malaki set his tea on the table so they could curl up together. "Okay, so what do you want to know?"

"Well, I have always wondered how a family of Samoans ended up in Washington."

"Oh, that's a boring story. My parents were both raised in America Samoa. My dad really didn't want to work in the tuna cannery. And other than working for the territorial government, there aren't any real prospects for success, so he joined the Army during

Vietnam. He managed to survive and they both earned their citizenship. After he was discharged, they settled in Washington." He chuckled. "He always said that he never wanted to see another Asian jungle again. So they moved to the most opposite climate they could think of."

"The Pacific Northwest?"

Malaki shrugged. "At least it wasn't Minnesota. And apparently, other than Hawaii and California, it has the biggest population of Pacific Islanders."

Javier picked up the remote and clicked on the TV. "Good to know. Oh, look, *Mean Girls* is on. And even though I hate it, I'll let you watch because it's your guilty pleasure and you're sick."

He slid down and rested his head on Javier's lap, not really caring what show his boyfriend put on, because chances were he was going to fall asleep again. Malaki sighed when Javier started to rub his shoulder and biceps.

"Have I told you lately how much I love your muscles?"

"Mmhm."

"So you know if you just lie here getting fat and lazy, I'm going to leave you, right?"

"Okay."

"I've been thinking of maybe a life change. How would you feel if I shaved my head, got a bunch of ink and started wearing tutus?"

"That's nice."

Javier chuckled. "You really are out of it, aren't you?"

"No, I'm ignoring your ridiculous ass. You say something that I think might be reasonably valid and I'll give you a real answer."

"Okay, okay. I'll stop messing with you. You just drink your tea and relax. Enjoy your show."

"I always did like the part where Regina says she has ESPN."

"That's Karen!"

Malaki snickered. "Yep, you totally hate this show."

"Shut up, Typhoid Mary."

* * * *

Javier peeked over his shoulder from his spot at the counter at Mal still asleep on the sofa. It had been a couple of hours and it was time to wake his lover up. The glow of the laptop screen cut through the dimness of living room. He'd kept the lights off for Mal's comfort, but there was enough light for him to still idly flip through the professional journal. He wasn't really reading the current research articles, but he'd already cleared out his emails, both work and personal. He no longer had any accounts on social media, in the effort to minimize his digital presence to anyone outside his immediate circle of friends. And there were only so many news source websites a person could review before they became irrevocably depressed.

"Hey, babe."

He jerked his head up and quickly lowered the screen of the laptop. "Hey, how are you feeling?"

Mal rubbed his hand over his face and top of his head. He grabbed one wrist and stretched his upper body with a loud groan. Javier smiled at the sound of Mal's shoulder cracking, because it proved the man actually was human. Also, despite the fact that he knew Mal wasn't trying to put on a show, he appreciated the reveal of skin and muscle beneath the hem of the T-shirt that was already stretched tight across Mal's torso.

"A lot better, actually. I probably won't sleep tonight since I've been sleeping all day."

"Hmm, well, if you hadn't been puking your guts out earlier, I might have a suggestion on how to burn off some extra energy."

"Extra energy might be a bit optimistic, but I'm going have to agree with you and say no sexy times tonight. What are you working on?"

"Nothing important. Just cruising viral cat videos on YouTube."

"You are the worst liar."

"I know."

Malaki sat in the chair next to him at the breakfast bar.

Javier patted Malaki's abs. "Think your stomach is up for a light late-night supper?"

"Yeah, maybe some soup. But you need to be getting to bed soon, since you have to work tomorrow. Are you going to stay?"

He nodded. "I was planning on it, unless you want to be alone. Please tell me you're taking at least one more day off."

Malaki pulled Javier's chair closer and wrapped his arms around him. "There is never a time I would rather be alone when I can be with you."

Javier snorted. "Just wait till the honeymoon phase wears off and I'm walking around the house farting and scratching my balls."

"I can't tell if you're serious or not."

"And that's the best part. But, seriously I can warm something up for you? I made myself some *pozole* earlier."

"Hmm, I might not be ready for pork, chili peppers, onion *and* garlic."

"Then I guess it's a good thing I also made a bland vegetable-only variety."

Malaki looked away and sighed.

"What's wrong?"

"Nothing. It's just it's been a long time since I had someone around to take care of me in any way and...I forgot how good it felt."

Javier smiled then made his way around into the kitchen. He'd kept the soup simmering on the stove, and pulled a bowl down from the cabinet. The scent of the soup suddenly made an old memory surface and he was transported to his *abuela's* kitchen. Javier probably hadn't been more than five or six, judging by his perspective and her smile. It wasn't until after his father had walked out that the smile had left her face. She'd stood near the stove ladling soup, and when Javier had turned around, he'd nearly gasped at the vision of his father sitting at the table. The man had pulled out the chair next to him and held out his arms. Javier had started towards his *papi*, but just before his felt his father's arms around him again, the memory faded and it was Mal's frown that came into focus.

"Hey, are you okay? You're breathing really fast. Maybe you should go back to your place. I don't want to spread any more germs to you than I already have."

Javier shook his head. "I'm fine, but thank you for asking. Just an old memory snuck up on me. Besides, I'm sure your germs are already multiplying by the millions inside me. It's up to my immune system now."

He set the bowl in front of Mal and crossed over to the fridge. He pulled open the door and the cool air swept across his flushed cheeks. He hadn't even been sure he remembered what his father looked like, but apparently an image had been locked in his subconscious somewhere. His pulse was racing and he couldn't seem to focus on the items inside to find what he'd gone there to search for to begin with.

"Turn around," Mal said softly.

Javier shifted and looked up. He didn't know why such an old memory had him all twisted up. He literally hadn't thought about his father in years. But it wasn't important. Mal was there in front of him, loving him for the man he'd become, and it was more important that Javier nurture the relationship that had healed his heart than chase a ghost.

"I mean it, Javi. I would feel a hundred times worse if I get you sick."

He wrapped his arms around his lover's neck. "We take care of each other, yeah? Some days I may need a little more help and others you, but that's part of figuring out this whole relationship thing together. It's the balance that makes us work."

"Look at that—you're not just a pretty face after all," Malaki said.

"Shut up, and now I'm going to risk my life and kiss you."

Because he needed Malaki's kiss more than anything in the world. And what were a few germs? Javier brushed his lips against the dry, warm skin of Malaki's cheek. He could still smell the soap Mal had used in his shower a few hours ago. Javier slid his lips against Malaki's, wishing he hadn't drunk the beer earlier so he wouldn't have any taste on his tongue but Mal's. He took his time, lingering over the slightly parted lips, licking at their curves, feeling Mal's gasping breath wash over his moist lips. Mal traced lines across his back and the mixture of his lover's hot touch and the cool air created a storm inside Javier that couldn't be controlled. He crushed their mouths together, invading forcefully, using his arms to encircle Malaki's waist and pull their bodies together tightly.

Mal moaned into Javier's mouth and gripped back of Javier's neck with one hand while using the other to pull their bodies closer together. They collided with the fridge door, and something rattled, bringing Javier to his senses. He tore his lips free and rested his forehead against Mal's chest.

"Sorry, I know you said you weren't up to sexual gymnastics."

Mal rubbed their groins together. He was just as hard as Javier, and it made Javier's cock twitch.

"Clearly, my cock has other ideas."

He didn't give Mal a chance to get out that infuriating 'but'. He captured his lips again in a continuation of the torrid kiss. What was it about Malaki's kisses that plugged the holes that life had ripped out of him? Javier wasn't a praying man, but if there was ever something to plead to a higher power it was that his love had the same ability for his man. Pushing his tongue into Malaki's mouth, Javier explored and stroked as the heat tumbled through him, ratcheting up the tension and anticipation in the air around them. He released Mal's neck, combing down the other man's back and pulling the T-shirt free of his waistband so he could touch the bare, warm skin at the base of his spine. Malaki took a couple of steps back, drawing Javier with him. Javier turned them so he could press Mal against the countertop, letting the fridge door swing shut.

He grabbed a handful of strongly muscled ass. Mal moaned and dove back into the hot, wet kiss with enthusiasm. He arched under Javier's hands as he sucked on his lower lip.

They were interrupted by a rather ominous growl coming from Mal's stomach. Javier backed off and looked down, unable to hold back a smirk. "I guess that means we should feed you after all."

Mal pulled him in against his body and Javier sighed at how such a simple gesture was able to even out the conflagration of emotions rioting inside him.

"Come on, big guy, let's get you rehydrated and fed. Then depending on how you tolerate anything in your stomach, maybe we can pick this up later."

He got busy getting a can of the Black Cherry Zevia that Malaki preferred when he wanted some bubbles from the fridge, and ladled a fresh bowl of soup from the pot on the stove.

"Hey, Javi?"

He carried his goods over to the table where Mal sat. "Yeah?"

"I love you."

The words were simple but carried with them the power to change worlds, and he respected that power. He treasured it even, and vowed to return it full force until it became inhumanly possible.

Chapter Fourteen

Javier stood near the counter at the place he liked to occasionally treat himself to for lunch. He was already anticipating the grilled chicken and brown rice wrap he'd ordered. He considered himself fortunate that the virus that had struck down Malaki last week had never made its effects known to him. Poor Mal had ended up being laid low for several days and had only made it back to work today. The man still looked at food with some trepidation. But Javier was starving and, now that he could eat without feeling guilty, planned to indulge in something totally decadent.

"Javier?"

He looked up at the kid behind the counter. "Thanks," he said, accepting the bag held out to him.

It was a short walk back to work and when he opened the front door, he saw a woman sitting on a waiting room chair. He didn't have any patients scheduled for another forty-five minutes and, as far as he knew, none of the other clinicians had appointments at this hour. He didn't see the clinic coordinator at her desk, which was unusual as they made it a policy to never leave it unattended.

"Can I help you?"

The woman stood, grasping the strap of her purse.

Javier did a five-point mental assessment and didn't notice anything immediately obvious about her posture that made it clear she was a patient.

"Are you Javier Alde?"

"Yes, do you have an appointment?"

"No, I'm not here for therapy. I'm here to see you."

She reached into her purse and Javier froze. When she pulled out an obviously tattered envelope, he nearly let out an audible breath.

"I found this letter when I was cleaning out my father's house. He's um, not well, and well, that's not important. Sorry. Um, let me start over. My name is Cecelia Pesano."

Javier dropped the sack and he was lucky he didn't have anything in his stomach, because he suddenly felt very ill. He started to back away towards the front door.

"Wait! I'm sorry I don't mean to bother you, but I'm hoping you can help me find my brother."

Javier stopped. "Help you find? Are you fucking with me? Leave me alone! What did you do with all the staff? Are you just like him?"

Cecelia looked around. "Like him how? Aren't the two of you, like, married? What staff? The place was empty when I came in."

He didn't even know how to respond. All he could do was stand there and shake his head. His brain unfroze and he looked down to realize he still had his phone in his hand. He kept his eyes on Cecelia and tried to unlock the screen at the same time. Her gaze moved down to his hands and she took a step forward.

"Don't come any closer. We never leave the front desk unattended."

"Okay. Okay. So I get the feeling that you and Luca aren't together." She held up the letter again. "This letter is a couple of years old, but he spoke of you with such love I just thought—"

"I'm going to be sick!" Javier pointed to the chairs "Sit."

He realized he'd barked quite loudly and the woman jumped. He tried to slow his breathing and tamp down the nausea.

"Please. I'm going to make some phone calls. Depending on what I find, I might be willing to talk to you."

She mouthed "*what the fuck*" as he moved over to the reception desk and put a barrier between him and the woman. He looked around for Kelsie and when she came around the corner from the hallway leading to the private treatment rooms, he sighed in relief.

"Who is that? There's nobody scheduled for another forty minutes. I had to use the potty."

"She's here to talk to me, but she's not a patient. Do me a favor, keep an eye on her while I make some calls?"

Kelsie gave him the side-eye. "Is everything okay?" she whispered.

"I'm not sure."

Javier dialed Agent Yang. When she picked up, he started talking right away. "Do you know if Vincent, sorry, Luca, had a sister? You never mentioned her as part of your investigation, but there's a woman sitting here in my waiting room claiming to have a letter from him addressed to their parents or something and wanting to talk to me. And part of me is compelled to listen in case there's some kind of clue why he fucked my life up so bad and the other part wants to run away screaming for the cops."

"Whoa, slow down, Javier."

"Sorry, sorry."

"It's okay. Now go back. You want to know if Luca Pesano had any siblings."

He nodded mutely, but realized that Agent Yang couldn't see him. "Yes."

"And I imagine you also want to know if this person claiming to be his sister may or may not have any criminal record?"

"That would be a good question too."

"So given that you are not law enforcement of any kind, I can't reveal any details we may have on an individual, but if you give me her name and general description, I can provide information about your reasonable safety."

"That's government speak for 'I can't tell you jack but I'm going to anyway', right?"

Agent Yang was silent and Javier accepted that as her acknowledgment. "She said her name is Cecelia Pesano. She's about five foot five, brown hair, dark brown eyes and average weight. Her accent is not Texan, but I couldn't tell you where it might be from. I could snap a photo and send it to you."

He did and received a slight frown from the woman sitting across the room, but Javier couldn't have cared less if she was offended that he was covering his ass. He messaged the photo to Agent Yang and heard the clicking sound of a keyboard.

"As far as I can tell, she matches the description of a half-sister on their father's side. But I'm afraid that's all I can say."

"Okay. I appreciate it. Listen, I don't want to seem overly paranoid, but can I text you in a little while if everything's okay? If you don't hear from me, send some kind of cavalry."

"That's fine. Also I would suggest you have someone nearby watch over the two of you. You don't have to talk to her, you know."

"I know, but at the same time, if she can provide any insight behind the why, it might help close the circle."

"I understand. It's one of the most elusive and heartbreaking questions we get asked. But I want you to prepare yourself for the possibility that the question may never be answered."

"I understand. Thanks for taking my call."

"Anytime."

Javier made another call to his therapist and they discussed the same possibility. Dr. Cappello said he would be available to see him later that evening if needed. He crooked his finger at Kelsie and she came towards him quickly, obviously having kept one ear on his side of the conversations.

"I'm going to take her into the office to talk. This is about something personal, but not exactly pleasurable."

"Say no more. I'll keep an eye out on the two of you and if your patient shows up early, I'll let you know."

"Thanks." He took a deep breath and let it out then walked back into the lobby. "Okay. I believe you are who you say, but I won't leave this building with you. My co-worker knows where we'll be."

Cecelia stood and held out the bag that Javier had dropped. "Here's your lunch."

Intellectually, he knew that it was unlikely she'd contaminated the food, but his gut wasn't willing to risk the possibility. Besides, he'd lost his appetite anyway. It didn't take long before Javier found himself sitting across a desk from the sister of a monster. It wasn't as though he wanted to assume she was just as evil. In fact, she seemed perfectly normal, but then again, so had Luca when they'd first met.

"How did you find me?"

She looked down at the crinkled letter and opened the flap. "I found this when I was cleaning out my father's house." She scoffed. "Father. That would imply that I had a relationship with the man, but in reality until a couple of weeks ago I hadn't seen him in twenty years. Anyway, it had your name and was postmarked Dallas, Texas. Google did the rest."

"Jesus. I both love and hate that thing. Agent Yang said that you were Luca's half-sister?"

"Agent who?"

"Yang. She's the FBI agent who led the investigation into your brother."

Cecelia's eyes went wide and she sat up straighter. "You called the FBI and told them I was here? Wait, what investigation?"

"Yes. And the investigation that focused on him being the prime suspect in the deaths of five people and the attempted murder of one more. Me." He could have been a little less cold, but he wanted to judge her reaction. Even if there was some slight condensing of the chain of events.

"Oh, holy fuck. Now I'm going to being sick." She let out a breath and looked away for a moment. "I just thought you might know how I could get in touch with him. To see if he wanted to get to know me. I had no idea…" She looked at Javier. "Now I get it, and I'm really sorry to bother you. I'll go."

Cecelia stood up and gathered her purse, but her hands shook as she gripped the strap. Unless she was the greatest actress in the world, the woman did not have a sinister plan to pick up where her brother had left off.

"Wait. Sit down." He stood and moved over to the other side of the desk. "Please."

Cecelia nodded and collapsed more than sat in the chair. Javier looked around for some tissues, but the best he had was a napkin from his lunch sack. He held it out to her and waited while Cecelia tried to catch the freight train he'd just sent her way.

"Tell me about what you *do* know and maybe we can help fill in some gaps for each other."

"Um, okay. Are you sure?" Javier nodded. "Luca and I share the same father, but different mothers. I was an accident. The byproduct of an affair. When my mother told Franco that she was pregnant, he said he would leave his wife and marry her. But that never happened. Instead his wife also happened to get pregnant with Luca around the same time."

"Sounds like a stellar guy."

Cecelia shrugged. "He ended up paying my mother to go away. When I was about ten, she took me to his work. I don't know if she was trying to get more money or actually get us to form some kind of relationship, but he acted like he didn't even know who she was. I saw a picture of Luca on his desk. That was basically the last time I saw him until recently. We never even spoke to each other."

"So how did you end up being the one to clean out his house?"

"I got a call from a case worker who's been helping him with his day-to-day stuff. She'd found contact information for me in his home office. I didn't even know he'd kept track of me all these years, but she said she found all kinds of stuff and a few photos. To be honest, I wasn't sure if it was a sign of some kind of repressed love or just creepy."

"That could definitely go either way."

"The case worker said he's been diagnosed with Alzheimer's and apparently his decline has been rather rapid. His wife passed a few years ago, and I just thought Luca was off the grid or something. I wanted to give him the chance to give input on what to do with the man. I'm certainly not capable of caring for him. I had no idea Luca was in prison."

Javier sat back in his seat and sighed. "He's not in prison."

"But you said…the FBI…and you. If he's not in… Oh."

"Yeah."

"When?"

"May twenty-first, 2017."

"You were there?"

"I was there. Do you want to know?"

She shook her head. "I don't think so. If what you say is all true, I think I'm better off not knowing anything more about him than I already do. He obviously was not the kind of person who I would have ever wanted in my life. I do have one question."

"Only one? I'm shocked."

A slight grin appeared and her eyes, which were eerily the same color as Luca's, twinkled.

"Do you know why? I mean was he sick? You know, like mentally ill or just a raging psychopath?"

"To be honest, I was hoping you might be able to help answer that. Luca held me captive and tortured me for seven months. The man I knew prior to being taken was clearly a façade, and I guess I was hoping you'd be able to fill in a lot of blanks about his history."

Cecelia started tearing up again and Javier once again hated that he'd atom-bombed the woman's hopes for the day.

"So you knew him? Before?"

Javier nodded. "I guess you could say we had dated."

"So my brother, and I even shudder a little bit calling him that now, kidnapped, tortured and tried to murder his boyfriend? No wonder you initially looked at me like I was the antichrist. How long were you together?"

Javier rubbed the back of his neck. "'Dated' and 'boyfriend' aren't exactly the right labels. Honestly, I think he was just an opportunist and sexuality didn't play a part in any of his choices. The details of our relationship probably cross into the area of 'you don't want to know.' But I respected him. I watched out for him. And, the day his mask came off was…well, shock would be putting it mildly."

"I guess this means neither of us are going to find what we're searching for today. This whole trip was a waste. I wish I had answers for you. I really do. And I feel like I should apologize to you for Luca's actions. Maybe I got lucky not growing up in that family? The old nature or nurture debate, you know?"

"I don't deny that our experiences shape us as individuals, but I also believe that there are just some people who have evil inside them. Regardless, don't apologize. I've never believed in that whole 'sins of the father' crap, or I guess brother in this case. Luca made his choices. I'm sorry I don't have any way of helping you get the answers *you* were looking for about either Luca or your father. Can I ask you a question?"

Cecelia shrugged. "Why not?"

"Was there anything that immediately stood out at your father's house that seemed like it belonged to Luca? An old bedroom or box of stuff?"

"Not that I noticed, but I haven't made it through the attic or basement yet. Why?"

"The case against him is closed, but Agent Yang is still working with the profilers who helped. Would you agree to let them on the premises? Maybe they might find insight or have questions we don't know about."

"Wouldn't they have done that during the investigation?"

"I don't know if they ever spoke to your father. And from what you're saying, he's incapable of providing information at this point. I just thought that maybe if there was some stuff lying around, it could help future cases that are similar."

"I'll have to think about it. You're right that my father can't make decisions anymore, but it's still his property."

"Fair enough. Since it's not an open investigation, I doubt they're going to come knocking with a warrant or anything. I'll give you Agent Yang's contact information and you can make that choice."

Cecelia nodded and stood. "I'm sure you have to get back to work. Sorry I ruined your lunch."

Javier held out his hand. "I wish it had been better circumstances, but it was nice to meet you. You didn't mention where you're from."

"I flew in from New York, but I live in Connecticut."

"Are you in town for long?"

"No, just a couple of days. I've never been to Texas, so I'll play tourist then find my way back home."

Javier reached across his desk and grabbed a sticky note. "Here's my cell and Agent Yang's," he said, scribbling out the numbers. "If you need anything while you're here, let me know."

Cecelia paused before taking the paper. "Thanks. I don't know why you're being so nice to me, but...have a good life, Javier. I really mean that."

"I'm trying. Each and every day."

He saw her out the back door and headed back to his office. Javier quickly glanced at his scheduling software to see if his next patient had arrived yet, but there wasn't a check mark by their name yet. He sat in his desk chair and unlocked his phone, immediately calling Mal.

"You are not going to believe what just happened."

"Your evil clone and his pet monkey just arrived from the future and claim they need you to sleep with a transgender stripper in order to save the planet or they will banish you to Buford, Wyoming with the Continuum Transfunctioner."

"I'm worried about the places your mind goes. No, a woman came by to see me. She was Luca's sister."

"What the fuck! Did you call the cops? Agent Yang? What did she want? Are you okay?"

He replayed the conversation for Malaki's benefit. "You know, the weird thing is that even though neither one of us got the answers we wanted, I definitely think she got the shittier end of the conversation."

"So do you feel better or was the whole situation just weird?"

"I don't know, a little of both maybe."

Kelsie hovered outside Javier's office door. "I'm sorry to bother you, but there are a couple of policemen out here who want to talk to you."

"Oh, crap, I forgot. I gotta run, the po-po are here. Probably going write me a ticket for crying wolf."

Kelsie pointed towards the waiting area then left, but not before Javier caught her little chuckle.

"Okay, I'll see you tonight?"

"Absolutely."

"Good. I have a whole week of misery to make up for and I need a good...cuddle."

"Mmhm? And would this cuddling involve any naked body parts?"

"It had better," Malaki growled.

"Then you better just consider me your little teddy bear."

"Oh, Javi, there is nothing little about you."

"Really, gotta go. Love you."

"Love you too."

He hung up and headed out to face the music. "I'm so sorry, Officers. I didn't really think Agent Yang was going to call in the cavalry so quickly. But I assure you that everything is okay."

"I'm sorry, what?"

"Agent Yang? FBI. Called you for a safety check because the sister of the man who held and tortured me for seven months dropped in unannounced and I kind of panicked? But it turns out everything is fine. She's not a narcissiopath like her brother. Well, half-brother apparently, and... You look like you have no idea what I'm talking about."

Both men shook their heads. One of them stepped forward and Javier looked at the patch with his last name stitched in bold white letters.

"Are you Javier Alde?"

"Yes, Sergeant Murphy, I am. If you're not here for the safety check, what are you doing here?"

"I'm sorry, sir, but we need to speak to you. Is there someplace with more privacy we can go?"

Javier glanced around the empty waiting room. "I'm fine here."

"Okay then, we need you to come identify a body."

"A what? Who?"

"Your mother, Salena Alde. I'm very sorry to tell you this, but she was found in her apartment this morning. Preliminary results suggest it was natural causes. I am very sorry for your loss."

The front door opened and Javier saw his first patient of the afternoon hobble in. *"Hola, Sr. Valdez, siéntese y estaré con usted en un momento."*

"Mr. Alde, did you hear what I said?" Sergeant Murphy asked.

"Yes, and I have questions. So many questions," he repeated in a whisper.

"I understand. If you'll come with us, we might be able to help. Can we give you a ride?"

"No, thank you. If you tell me where I need to go, I'll stop by after work."

Sergeant Murphy took a few steps forward and indicated for Javier to move out of the open area of the waiting room. "Mr. Alde, do you understand what we are telling you?"

"Yes, Sergeant. I understand English just fine, contrary to what you may assume."

"That's not what I... Mr. Alde, your mother – "

"See, let me stop you right there. I'm going to set aside the question of how you came to the conclusion of my alleged connection to this woman. You stated that you have a woman identified as Salena Alde in the morgue and you'd like me to come see if she is the same woman who gave birth to me. The same woman who, last time we spoke, told me I was an abomination and would burn in hell. She completely excised me from her life and last I'd heard was no longer even living in the US. So I will finish my scheduled appointments for the day because my patients need me, and most of them volunteer their gratitude on a daily basis. After my responsibilities have been met, I will do as you request, but please consider I haven't seen my mother in a nearly a decade, so this woman may not match the one in my memories."

The other officer cleared his throat and held out a business card. "This is the medical examiner's information. You can call when you're ready to come down. I'm sure he'll be flexible to your schedule. We'll be on our way so as not to disrupt your patients any further."

"Thank you for your understanding."

The one who'd offered him the card nodded and grabbed his partner by the arm when the man opened his mouth to no doubt give Javier another piece of his mind. Clearly his lack of grief confounded the man. But he didn't really care. It wasn't as if he had to justify his feelings to a complete stranger.

He popped his head around the corner and saw Mr. Valdez check his watch. *"Siento la tardanza. Sólo uno más momento y yo estaremos con usted."*

Javier quickly send Malaki a text.

Hey, love. Change of plans. Meet me at work when you're done and we need to run an errand. I'm going to need you to drive because I plan on getting drunk…very drunk tonight.

* * * *

Javier opened the door to the medical examiner's office. With each step towards the desk in the middle of the lobby, the goosebumps on his skin seemed to grow. Mal's hand on his lower back chased away some of the chill, but Javier still felt there was more ice than blood running through his veins.

"Can I help you?"

Javier tried to hide the tremor in his hands by gripping the edge of the counter. "My name is Javier Alde. I have an appointment with the medical examiner."

"Yes, sir. I'll let Dr. Liefson know you're here."

"Thank you." He turned to look at Mal. "Why am I so nervous?"

"Because you're about to see your mom for the first time in nine years. It's perfectly normal to feel some uncertainty."

"If she were alive, I would totally buy into that. But my mom is reportedly dead. So it's not as if anything is really going to change in my life. All I need to do is look at...look at a body, and tell them if...if it's her."

"Mr. Alde, I'm Dr. Liefson, the chief medical examiner for Dallas County. Thank you for coming down. I'm sorry it's under these circumstances."

The doctor stood tall. His black suit said *consummate professional* but the deep purple sneaks with coordinating checked shirt and tie said he had personality. Javier shook his hand, "Yes, well, as I told the officers who came to my work, I haven't had any contact with Salena Alde in almost a decade. I'm not entirely sure what information I have that will be helpful to you."

"Come with me, please."

They followed Dr. Liefson through the lobby, ran a maze of hallways and down a floor until they came to a set of doors leading to the morgue. Javier knew because it said so, but it might have been his imagination that made it seem as if they were blinking in neon colors. They went through the doors, but instead of finding himself faced with rows of metal cabinets that held bodies, Javier and Mal entered an office.

"Okay, so if you don't want an up-close view I can project the table onto the LCD screen here."

He glanced over at the bookcases and credenza that took up one entire wall, and sure enough, there was a decent-sized TV hanging on the wall right in the middle.

"What do you want, Javi?"

On one hand, he wanted to get this over as fast as possible, but on the other… "If this really is the last time I'll ever see her, I think I want to do it in person."

Dr. Liefson nodded. "I understand. Come this way."

There was another door in the corner that Javier hadn't noticed before, but when he passed through, it was as if he'd entered another world, cold and sterile where the office had been warm and homey. He shivered and leaned in to Malaki's arm around him. His eyes were glued to the body-shaped sheet seemingly hovering in the air. As they got closer Javier noticed smells. Some were familiar as generic medical scents, but others cluttered his sinuses in a way that he knew wouldn't dissipate until long after the day ended.

Dr. Liefson pulled back the sheet to reveal a woman's face. As Javier stared down, he tried to catalog features that should be familiar. The black hair was shorter than he remembered, but the deep-set eyes and narrow lips matched his memories. The one obvious element that was wrong was her skin color. Instead of the tawny beige color highlighted with rose undertones, the body in front of him had a blueish-purple marble-like appearance.

"It's her." He looked up at the medical examiner. "Can you tell me anything about her?"

"She died of a massive pulmonary embolism."

"A blood clot?"

"Yes. The officers mentioned on the phone that you had not seen your mother in a very long time?"

Javier nodded "Almost ten years. Is there anything else you can tell me? Where did she live? Work?"

"I'm sorry. I only know what was in the police report. She was found in an apartment in the Urban Park neighborhood. I'm sure the detectives assigned to the case can answer your questions."

He shook his head. "It doesn't really matter, I guess."

A single tear found its way down his cheek unchecked. And as if it called out to the universe in its loneliness, the flood gates opened and Javier screamed out years of pain, unanswered questions, self-loathing and regret. He sought shelter against Malaki, unmindful of the tears that soaked his shirt.

"I've got you, Javi. Just let it all out."

He tried to put his arms around Mal, but his limbs suddenly weighed a hundred pounds each and hung at his sides. The air behind him moved and his ears rang with the sound of metal sliding on metal. He looked up just as Dr. Liefson shut the door of the cooler with a resounding *click*. When he was able to stand on his own he turned around, trying to appear composed, but undoubtedly looking a muddled, snot-nosed mess.

"What do I do now?"

That was a question with so many interpretations, and he was in no place to even contemplate half of them.

"With her, I mean?"

"That's up to you. You are under no obligation to claim the body."

"If I don't, what will happen to her?"

"You have twenty-seven more days to make a decision. If more than thirty days pass and a body remains unclaimed, they are cremated and the county disposes of them in a local cemetery."

"Okay, I don't know what to do right now."

"I can understand that. You know how to reach me when you do."

He turned to look at Mal. "Can we go now?"

"Yeah, love. We can go. I called Brandon and Tyler on my way to pick you up and they should be in the city about now. How does some top shelf tequila sound?"

"Like the answer to all my prayers."

Malaki nodded to Dr. Liefson and Javier followed his lead back up to the lobby. Where before his body had practically vibrated, now numbness pervaded. He came to when the metallic black of Malaki's truck door swarmed his vision.

Mal turned Javier around and cupped his cheek. He bent down and when their lips touched, it was like a jolt from an AED. Life suddenly filled him again. Fortunately, that life belonged to the man he loved with all his heart.

"Oh, Javi. I'm so sorry," Malaki said when they parted.

"You know, it's strange? I shouldn't feel sad. Not really. Like I said, it's not as if losing her is going to change anything. So why does it hurt so much?"

"Maybe because where before somewhere in your subconscious, there was a glimmer of hope that someday the two of you might reconcile, now the story of your relationship has truly ended."

Javier shrugged. "Maybe. Let's go get drunk. Well, I'll get drunk. I'm just going to apologize in advance for you having to deal with me later."

Malaki kissed him softly. "No apology necessary. Now let's go."

Chapter Fifteen

"I'm sorry, but you mean to tell me that your mother has been living in Dallas all this time? Was living? Had lived? I probably could have figured that out two shots ago."

Javier saluted Brandon then swallowed another shot of tequila. "Apparently."

Their little party had made liberal use of the happy hour specials. Or at least he and Brandon had. *God bless his mate for sacrificing his liver on behalf of their friendship.*

"What a bitch."

Tyler squeezed Brandon's hand while he sipped his beer.

"Sorry," Brandon mumbled

Javier shrugged. "It's not something I haven't already said."

"So what did the police have to say?" Tyler asked.

"We only talked to the medical examiner. He said they've actually had her down in the morgue for three days while they tried to find next of kin. They ended up tracking me down because of my birth certificate on file with the records office. They also apparently found my parents' marriage license and record of divorce."

"Did they try to find your dad?"

He rolled his beer bottle between his hands. Mal's big body took up more than his share of the booth, and if Javier didn't think it would completely emasculate him, he would probably have laid his head on his lover's shoulder.

"Javi?"

He looked up at the group. "Huh?"

"Did they try to locate your dad?"

"Oh, um, I don't think so. I don't know really. Haven't talked to any of the investigators yet."

"What do we need to do for a funeral?" Tyler asked.

"What funeral? The woman abandoned him—he can do the same," Brandon said.

"While that may be true, she was still his mother," Mal added.

"Okay, I feel like I have three Jiminy Crickets sitting beside me right now."

"I have always wanted to wear a top hat and tails," Brandon said.

"I'll keep that in mind for the wedding," Tyler said with a smile.

Brandon choked on a sip of his drink and started coughing. "Excuse me?"

Javier couldn't help but smile at the mixture of pure terror and longing in Brandon's gaze.

"You know, Zach's wedding. The one we're groomsmen for."

"Oh…right. *Zach's* wedding. Although I don't really think your brother's looking to our input for the wedding attire. In fact, I question whether Zach has much input on his own code of dress. If I hear him say 'as you wish' one more time to that gorgeous creature who is way too good for him, I will escalate from rolling my eyes behind his back to outright mocking him."

Tyler chuckled. "That's a bit of an exaggeration."

Brandon stared Tyler down. "Really?"

Tyler tilted his head and stared off into the middle distance. "Well, you might be right. But he loves her, so he just wants her to be happy."

"I know, and they're perfect together. But it's still my right as his pseudo brother-in-law to make fun of him."

"What if we made it not so pseudo?"

Javier's buzz vanished in an instant and Malaki gripped his leg underneath the table. Was Tyler proposing? Right here? He'd always figured the man would make a big production out of the occasion whenever the time came, but then again Brandon wasn't exactly one for flash mobs and giant balloon drops.

"Are you fucking with me?" Brandon asked.

"No. Will you marry me?"

Javier found himself holding his breath. Brandon loved Tyler with his whole heart, but Brandon did have a stubborn streak and might fight the notion of marriage not because of their relationship, but simply due to the institution.

"What are the terms?"

"You and me forever. What I have is yours and likewise. I will never prevent you from being your own man, but I'm hoping we'll find a way to grow together. If you'd like a bit more pomp and circumstance, I can get all the servers over here to sing a song and bring a piece of cake with a sparkler candle."

"I don't think that will be necessary," Brandon said as he dug into his pocket. "but we might need one of these." He held up a wedding band that glistened in the lighting.

Tyler reached into his jeans pocket. "Or two of them."

"Seriously, you two?" Javier exclaimed. "You've just been carrying those around in your pants? What if you tried to find some change and they fell out? Or you tossed your clothes in the washer, but forgot they were in there?"

"Um, Javi?" Malaki whispered.

He looked over at his partner. "What? You know what I'm getting at. I figured they were going to get around to this eventually, but either they are the worst communicators in the world or share the same brain. Since Tyler asked first, does that mean that Brandon's proposal is void? Or would they cancel each other out and be right back where we all started when we sat down?"

Brandon and Tyler both started snickering, which turned into outright laughs.

He glared across the table. "What is so funny, you freaking hyenas? This is a big deal even if you want to pretend it's not."

"Should we put him out of his misery?" Brandon asked

Tyler slid the smoke-colored ring he held onto Brandon's finger and Brandon eased the black metal one onto his.

Javier blinked several times. "What is happening?"

"Tyler asked me last weekend. We were coming to share the news with you and our folks."

"That was why we were already on our way to the city when Malaki called that you needed some cheering up."

Javier sniffed and tried to hide the fact that his eyes were tearing up for the first time since seeing his mother's body. "You assholes. I love you." He raised his beer. "Just because our past didn't turn out like we wanted doesn't mean our future can't be better than we ever imagined. To Brandon and Tyler."

"To Javier and Malaki," Brandon added.

Malaki gripped Javier's hand and held it against his chest. "May we always have happiness to uplift us, trials to keep us strong, success to keep us eager, faith in each other and determination to face another day."

"Now that I'll drink to." Tyler wrapped his arm around his fiancé and planted a kiss on Brandon's temple.

* * * *

Malaki rolled over in bed and flung his arm over Javi's waist. His lover's soft snuffles made him smile. The man hated to admit it, but after getting his drink on there was always snoring. However, Malaki completely understood the need for some alcoholic numbness after the day Javier had had. After they'd left the restaurant, he'd brought Javi home and, while his lover was dead to the world, Malaki was finding the Land of Nod elusive.

Listening to Javier recount his and Cecelia's talk, then learning about the new level of coldness with which Javier's mother had abandoned him gotten Mal thinking a lot about family — the family that one was born into and the family one made. He'd been so fortunate that his parents and sister were still an important part of his life. But he could do more to strengthen their bonds. It wasn't that he avoided the town he'd grown up in, but admittedly he had been rather selfish in not taking the time to go home at least occasionally.

"Hey, Javi?" he whispered.

There was no response. He tapped the sprawled body lying next to him "Javi?" he tried again.

Nothing. Malaki leaned back and gave Javier a good shove. Javier snorted and shuffled over onto his side away from Malaki. He recoiled and tried to act like nothing happened. "Hey, Javi?"

"Bwah?"

"I think we should go to my parents' for Christmas."

"Mmkay."

"Really? You'll come with me to Everett?"

"I'll go with you to Mars if you let me get back to sleep."

He slid his hand around Javi's hip and cupped his soft cock. "I *could* let you sleep...or...I could suck your cock."

Javier stiffened for the briefest of seconds and Mal thought he was about to get the 'I have a headache' excuse for the first time in their relationship. It was completely reasonable, but an ache settled in his chest all the same. Then Javi arched into his grip.

He loved the feel of Javier's cock in his hand, even in its most relaxed state. The weight of his slowly awakening flesh in his palm stirred his blood in a different way than when they came together in a rush. His body responded in kind as he brought Javier to full mast. He used his other hand to stroke Javier's stomach. The muscles beneath his fingers twitched. He skimmed his fingers over the scarred ridges, but when Mal pressed down, the flesh settled and Javier let out a soft breath.

"What do you want? I'll give you anything your heart desires," Malaki whispered.

"I want our lives, yours and mine, to mean something more than just a notation in history that we survived."

He turned Javier over so he was lying on his back and Malaki could see his face. "Oh, babe. That's already true. You want to know why?"

Javier nodded and rolled a little closer to Malaki.

"Because when two people share the kind of love that we do, they become more than a footnote in the tomes of history. They change it. *We* change it."

He kissed Javier. Kissed him in a way that was more than physical. More than two people expressing their love for each other. His kiss was a soul promise. The promise to both his lover and the universe that this mark in the fabric of time was more than a mere thread — it was the binding that wove two souls together. He and Javier might not be world leaders. They might not perform great deeds of heroism, but as a unit, the two of them still had the power to change lives for the better, thereby creating a ripple effect expanding to many, far and wide.

He rolled them so that Javier was on top, savoring the feel of his man above him, the heavy weight of muscle and bone pressing him into the mattress. He loved it when Javier used his strong fingers to knead his flesh in a way that sparked thousands of tiny fireworks beneath his skin.

"Methinks it's actually you who wants to get fucked." Javier took Malaki's nipple between his teeth.

Mal gasped and arched against Javier's mouth. "Yes…please fuck me, Javi."

Javier sat up, licking his lips. Even in the dark, his eyes looked dazed.

"Get the lube."

Mal yanked open the drawer and shoved his hand inside, blindly fumbling for the bottle he'd bought just the other day.

Javier maneuvered his way down and took Mal's cock in his mouth. The feel of warm, wet suction consumed all Mal's thought process.

"I love the feel of you in my mouth. Love these sparse indigo strands at the base of your cock and the scent of your flesh here on your inner thighs and sac."

Mal's balls tightened and he clenched his hands, one in the bedcovers and the other successfully around the treasure he sought in the drawer.

He held up the bottle. "I'm going to come if you keep that up."

Javier snatched the bottle from Mal's hand, clicked the cap open and poured a generous amount into his palm. "Well, that *is* the plan, but I think my cock might be disappointed if it doesn't get to be part of the game."

Hooking his hands behind his knees, Malaki pulled his legs up and apart, exposing himself completely. "I want you bare."

Javier stilled, his eyes wide and his breath quickening. "Are you sure?"

"Never more." They'd both gotten tested some months ago, but had agreed to wait for this step until absolutely sure it was more than their hormones making the decision. Everything they'd experienced today indicated to Malaki that it was time.

Javier bent over and rested his forehead on Malaki's stomach. The warmth of his breath was directly opposite to the cool, slippery fingers rimming his hole. Javier pushed his fingers inside him and all higher functioning abandoned Malaki's brain. "Fucking hell,

Javi." He tried to breathe and concentrate on holding his legs as high up and as far apart as he could. It was only two fingers so far, but felt like so much more. He started to close his eyes, but a quick nip from Javier's teeth had them flying open.

"I want you to watch me. Watch how the two of us come together. I love how tight and soft you are."

The way Javier was kneading his sweet spot and working himself into Mal's ass was slowly driving him mad. He licked his dry lips and tried to speak, but the words came out more like a frog's croak. "I need more."

Javier's effort to hold back was evident from the sweat beading on his forehead. Why was he torturing them both? Javi knew he loved a good, strong fuck. He gloried in the moments when his boyfriend let those toppy muscles flex, just as much as he savored the times when Javier would seek out Mal's quiet support after a hard day.

Javier leaned down and flicked his tongue across the tip of Mal's cock. "I can give you more. I'll give you everything." The words could have been said in jest, but they carried a far greater weight. He was having trouble remembering how to talk and it wasn't just because Javier was lighting up his flesh with his magical touch. The dark intensity of Javier's gaze shining up at him had him hypnotized.

Javier twisted his fingers and moved them apart inside him. "Oh, fuck yes." He couldn't hold Javier's gaze any longer. Malaki stared up at the ceiling of his bedroom. Tiny gasps and groans were all he got out as he tried to articulate the sensations spreading throughout his body.

"That's it, Mal. God, I love the way you come apart for me."

Javier had reached deep, twisting and scissoring his fingers as he pumped Malaki's ass in a slow, steady motion. His prostate sang with each touch of Javi's long fingers. Mal's heart pounded and his toes curled. He needed Javier inside him and he needed it now. "Please."

"Just the thought of sliding into you, skin to skin, has me on the verge of coming."

Javier swooped over him and claimed Malaki's mouth in a punishing kiss. He instantly missed his lover's fingers, and a pathetic whimper may have escaped. Javier sat, picking up the lube. There was a slight tremor in his fingers as he slicked up his rigid cock. He licked his lips as a drop of precum slid down over Javi's fingers. Javier poised himself at Mal's entrance.

"Put your legs on my shoulders."

Javier dropped his gaze, focusing between Malaki's legs with such intensity it was like another touch. Javier rocked his hips, and the feel of his naked cock pushing inside him had Malaki holding his breath. While the motions might have been the same as countless other times they'd made love, Malaki couldn't help but feel there was a whole new element to their joining. With an aching slowness, Javier entered him. Mal clenched down instinctively as he realized that nothing separated their bodies.

"*Oh, Dios mío.*" Javier's breath hitched. "So hot, so slick. I really didn't think it would be that different, but holy fuck, you have got to try this. I've gotta move."

Yes, fuck yes, move, move-move-move!

He couldn't seem to get the words out, so Malaki tried to speak with his body. He wrapped his legs around Javier's waist and lifted his hips. The movement forced

Javier's cock deeper inside him. Their groans mingled in the darkened room. Malaki's blood raced, but a peacefulness infiltrated his muscles. Their limbs were tangled and, beneath Malaki's palms, Javier's back rippled as he traced the lines of muscles. Javier shifted his weight and the space between their upper bodies became nearly non-existent.

He sought out the tender spot on Javier's jaw, kissing the pulsing vein. Javier's arms partially collapsed and his belly rubbed against Malaki's dripping cock, sending sparks of fire through him. Javier liked to give Mal trouble for living such a clean lifestyle, but his lover didn't realize that Mal didn't have any room for any other vices. Javier was the one addiction he couldn't live without, and he had no intention of seeking treatment.

He slid his hands up Javier's slick chest. Javier pulled partway out of Malaki's ass, then shoved back in. The head of his cock hit Mal's gland both ways, causing him to gasp. "Javi…"

"I've got you, *mi vida*."

Mal might have been the larger of the two of them, but, in moments like these, it was as if Javier became superhuman. He adjusted his hands and lifted Mal's hips. Within a few heartbeats, Javier had him moaning and clutching at the blankets.

"I feel you, *corazón*. Your heat wrapped around me. Every ripple massaging my cock."

Time slowed and instead of seconds or minutes, Mal marked the progression of each moment by the deep moans that sounded out and the contractions of his muscles. Each drive of Javier's hips hurled him deeper into the gravitational vortex of ecstasy.

"Mal?"

"I...fuck, Javi...so damned close."

Javier dropped onto his elbows, their muscles straining as their bodies slid against each other. He clamped around Javier, and with the tiniest change of angle Javier sent Mal hurling towards oblivion.

"I can feel you. Holy shit, I can feel everything."

His entire existence narrowed down to Javier and the sight of him coming undone, the scent of their desire, and the arousal spiraling tighter and tighter within him. Their bodies moved in a beat only they heard, but the maelstrom of pleasure threatened to consume him. He sought out the sanctuary of his lover, begging the man to lead him to safety. Javier, as always, read him with the authority of a virtuoso. He hitched Mal's legs up, setting a pounding pace. Mal couldn't hold off any longer.

He reached between them, stroking his own shaft. Each drag of his hand up and down his cock had him arching his back and moaning as he pleaded with the universe for that one last sensation that would send him falling into the abyss of pleasure.

Javier shifted his weight, and he shoved Mal's hand aside. Javi stroked Mal's cock hard and fast, twisting around the head just the way he liked. He dug into Javier's sweat-soaked skin, while planting his other hand on the headboard behind him just in time to keep Javi's powerful thrusts from knocking his head against the metal frame. He stared up into Javier's eyes.

"Come around me."

Javier nailed Mal's gland and his thumb tapped his slit. Mal couldn't stop the shout as his cock shot a splash of hot liquid on his stomach. His hole convulsed, his insides constricting around Javi's shaft. Javier's cry of completion mixed with his own. Javier's cock swelled and a rhythmic pulse signaled that his lover was unleashing a torrent of cum.

Javier froze for a long moment, eyes closed and breathing rapid, before he collapsed on top of Mal. Malaki wrapped his arms around the man who held his heart in his hands. He pulled Javi close, stroking his back. Mal's body still strummed with the echoes of pleasure that he'd do everything in his power to experience for the rest of his life.

"So, think you can fall asleep now?" Javier asked.

Mal chuckled. "That obvious, was I?"

Javier scooched up till he nestled his head in the crook of Mal's neck. "Yes, I could hear you thinking even in my sleep." He propped his head on his hands. "Did you mean it?"

He loved it when Javi camped out on him like his personal mattress. His lover wasn't a slight man by any means, but Mal couldn't think of anything better than the warm weight of Javier's body against him.

"Mean what?"

"Taking me home to meet your family?"

"One hundred percent. I think it's time, don't you? If they hadn't spoken to you on the phone and FaceTime, they'd probably think you were a figment of my imagination."

"I'm nervous. I mean I'm excited too, but I think meeting them makes them more real."

"And let me guess, you're afraid of losing another family if you really let them in?"

"There are no guarantees, Mal. Sometimes love really isn't enough to hold two people together. If we don't work out, you clearly have dibs on them."

He rolled them so he covered Javier. "You're right. There are no guarantees in life. A very wise man once told me that you never see the difficult moments in a photo album. It's all smiles and laughter, but love is the adhesive that gets you from one snapshot to the next. Before you know it, you have fifty years of photos to look through."

"Ridiculously cheesy, but there might be a bit of truth in there. Who told you that?"

"My dad. The first time I told him that I'd fallen in love with you."

Chapter Sixteen

"So, is your mom going to bust out the baby album this week?" Javier asked as they made their way through the terminal at SeaTac Airport.

They'd had to fly into Seattle and would make the thirty-minute or so drive north to Malaki's hometown of Everett by car. Mal's dad had offered to pick them up, but they wanted to have access to a car without being an inconvenience to his family.

They stepped outside and Javier took his first breath of Pacific Northwest air. Since they were in the city, it didn't seem all that different from Dallas. Less dry, but still urban. He shivered as cool damp air hit his neck. *Okay, maybe it's different.*

"Let's go get our car, then I'll get you out of this rat race and into the mountains where we can breathe."

Javier pulled his suitcase and followed Mal, who thankfully knew where to go. They had to catch a shuttle bus over to the rental car facility, which was like a giant terminal of its own. At least everything was very well labeled and the process was smooth. Before long, they were secured in their upgraded SUV.

"I was thinking of maybe taking the scenic route to my parents' place. That way you can see some of the countryside. Unless you'd rather get there the quickest way possible?"

He leaned over the console and pulled Mal down for a thorough kiss. It had been hours since they'd really touched, and as they were on vacation, Javier had every intention of letting himself enjoy each moment.

"What was that for?"

"Because I can."

"Well, then, I can think of some creative way to use this giant back seat."

The gleam in Mal's eyes almost had him removing his seatbelt and jumping out of the car, but they were still in a very public, very large parking lot.

"Maybe later we can sneak out and act like hormone-riddled teenagers. And I'd love to take the long way. Maybe get some fresh air, since my lungs and skin have just about dried out from all the recycled oxygen."

"I know what you mean. We're going to get back to Dallas looking ten years younger."

Mal navigated his way out of the airport. But aside from a really huge-ass lake they drove past, Javier didn't think Seattle was anything to write home about. They'd been driving for about twenty-five minutes when the urban landscape fell away and he found it difficult to keep his head from swiveling with each mile that passed.

Javier had never seen so many green trees in his life. The tips of the pines seemed to reach to the sky and the branches held out their arms, locking away the secrets of the forest from casual observer.

"So where are you — oh, my God, it's snow," he whispered.

"Yeah. Up in the mountains, it can snow as early as October, but in town snowfall is rare. We mainly just get rain. Wait — have you never seen snow before?"

Javier shook his head.

"But you've seen mountains, right? When you traveled for games with A&M?"

"No, we never traveled to anywhere north of Kentucky."

"Oh, shit. That does it — at some point this week, we're really getting up into the mountains, assuming the passes aren't closed. Right now, I'm taking you to the nearest waterfall I can think of. We'll see the peaks, but not from the summit. But once we do...oh, Javi, the views will make you catch your breath, and at night I swear you can reach right out and touch the stars. It's funny — I don't really miss this place when I'm gone, but now that I'm back, it's like I can't wait to show you all the amazing things it has to offer."

"Makes sense. You've roamed far and wide, but this will always be home."

Malaki turned to Javier when they came to a stop sign. "Yes, I'm excited for you to get the chance to finally meet my family, but our life together is what home means to me."

Javier grasped Mal's hand. "When you suggested we make this trip, I could tell how important it was to you, and I'm happy to celebrate the holiday with your family. But I want you to know that you and our life together is what I'm most thankful for this year."

Javier jumped when a loud horn went off behind them, making him and Malaki laugh. Mal turned the car and he saw a sign for the parking area for

Snowqualmie Falls. He knew he should be trying to play it cool, but he couldn't help but be a little antsy in his seat. He'd never seen a real mountain waterfall before.

As he stepped out of the car, he was hit with the scent of pine. He closed his eyes and sighed as cool, moist air blasted his skin.

"You ready? It's about a half mile to the base of the falls."

"Let's go."

The trail was obviously well maintained and marked, making it clear that this was a popular tourist destination during nice weather. However, since it was only about forty degrees, foggy and raining off and on today, they had the place to themselves. He decided to enjoy the moment and took Malaki's hand. The fog floating through the trees could have lent an eerie atmosphere, but instead a sensation of familiarity pervaded. He looked down at his and Malaki's joined fingers as they walked in silence.

They exited the forest and the trail changed from compacted dirt to a planked boardwalk. They wound around the side of the mountain and came to a platform. Ahead of him were the falls. The sound of the water pounding on the rocks drowned out the thoughts scrambling in his brain. The spray floating through the air mixed with the fog and obscured the details of the cliffs. He loved Texas, the arid land in the western part of the state and the granite and prickly pear cactus of the hill country, but as he looked around he could understand why the unique beauty of this land called to people.

"You know what I love the most?" Malaki asked

He shook his head.

"I love how the violent pounding of the water freefalling over the cliff turns into this peaceful water flowing calmly right below us."

Life. The rapids you're unsure if you'll survive, the freefall of the unknown, the sometimes crushing brutality, but if you're lucky, you can find someone to help you navigate the uncharted terrain and find the peaceful waters.

He looked up at Mal. "So what do you say we explore those waters together?"

Their lips met at the moment the sun broke through. Javier smiled as prisms of colors danced in the air over their heads. He took Mal's hand and led him towards the path into the unknown.

Want to see more from this author? Here's a taster for you to enjoy!

Turkish Delights
Trina Lane

Excerpt

Garrett glanced up from his laptop and looked around the business class cabin of the airplane. All seemed to be in order, but something had caught his attention. Then he saw out of the corner of his eye, one row back on the opposite side, a man had spilled his drink and was frantically trying to wipe the mess off his dress shirt.

Good luck, bloke. Hope you have a spare.

Garrett had learned the hard way to have a backup shirt and tie easily accessible when traveling for work. He turned his attention back to his laptop screen and clicked Play on iTunes. He always made sure to have music on his flights. There was nothing worse than listening to the incessant drone of jet engines — especially when he had this much work that needed to be done. He blinked a few times as the images on his screen blurred. A cup of tea would really be brilliant about now.

Garrett had checked in at Heathrow at five o'clock that morning for his flight at seven. Of course that meant he'd actually left his flat in Epsom at four. He was a well-seasoned traveler, not unused to early or late flight times, but considering he'd only gotten two hours of sleep last night, Garrett was knackered. Garrett's boss had called him to say that the officers and board of Totally Five Star Hotels, the company he worked for, had called a late meeting yesterday. They wanted to make significant changes to the design of their newest hotel in the thirteenth hour.

The flight from London to Istanbul was nearly half over, and while he would love to have a lie-down, there was simply too many items still on his checklist before landing. The newest property was scheduled to break ground in a matter of a couple of weeks, and it was now up to him to break the news of the changes to Kyle LaFleure, the primary architect on the project. Kyle had already been in transit to Istanbul when Garrett's boss had called the meeting. Garrett knew that Kyle was not going to be happy. He'd already spent months drafting and finalizing the blueprints for the hotel. They'd already gotten approval from the building inspector, municipality, infrastructure departments, and had obtained their building permits. Basically, they'd now have to start from scratch.

Garrett rubbed his temples as a headache threatened. He wasn't even sure if his boss's ideas were viable for the lot they'd purchased. He sensed many long, late nights working with Kyle in his future. That wouldn't necessarily be a bad thing, because Kyle was bloody gorgeous, but Garrett had a strict hands-off policy when it came to co-workers. The last few months working with the Frenchman had significantly tested Garrett's resolve. It certainly didn't help matters that he'd caught Kyle glancing in his direction on more than one occasion, either. Garrett jerked his head up quickly when someone touched his shoulder.

"Can I get you anything, sir?"

Garrett removed his ear buds. "A cup of tea? Please?"

The flight attendant walked off and Garrett dug a tiny bottle of painkillers from his laptop case—another thing he'd learned never to travel without. He placed the small capsules on his tray table then looked back at his notes. The proposed changes were complex, but if possible, they would ensure that the new hotel would be the ultimate Ottoman luxury experience, which, of course, was the goal. Since being named European Capital of Culture two years ago, Istanbul had become the fifth most popular tourist destination in the world. According to the demographics Garrett had gathered in preparation for the project, eleven point six million foreign visitors arrived each year—partially due to the city's historical draw, but increasingly due to its emergence as a major cultural and entertainment hub.

"Here you are, sir," the attendant said as she set his tea down.

"Thank you. I might just survive now."

He popped his painkillers and sighed as the warm brew fed stimulants to his veins. Garrett knew he had to have everything organized for his meeting with Kyle this afternoon, and with the pharmaceutical assistance, Garret should be able to get himself back on track.

* * * *

Garrett gathered his carry-on and made his way off the plane. The local time was almost one in the afternoon. His meeting with Kyle was scheduled for three. Fortunately, his company had arranged for a car service to take him from Atatürk Airport to Beyoğlu. They'd also taken care of leasing a flat and a car since he'd be in Turkey for the duration of the project. He was supposed to pick up the car from the leasing office in the morning.

Garrett followed the signs to passport control for other nationalities after retrieving his checked luggage. He'd applied for his extended visit visa before leaving the UK. Since he'd already been to Turkey several times in preparation for the project, Garrett was familiar with which queues to enter. It seemed as if there was light traffic this afternoon, which was very relieving. He made his way up to the counter and handed over his documents to the agent. Garrett watched as the agent slowly entered his information into the computer system then stamped his passport without interest. He nodded his thanks then retrieved his identification. He collected his luggage after checking the monitors for the proper carousel then headed toward customs. Garrett didn't have to do a spot check, so he quickly entered the arrivals hall. He looked around for the car service driver. He'd been told there would be someone holding up a sign with his name on it, but it was hard to see through the hundreds of travelers dodging each other and toting luggage through the terminal. An older gentleman nearly collided with Garrett, but must have felt that the near accident was Garrett's fault, because he started waving his arms and cursing at him in Turkish. Garrett had picked up a few phrases on his previous trips and didn't appreciate the man's comments about his mother.

There was another bloke dressed in a black suit running toward the customs area. Garrett watched until the man skidded to a stop, looking around the terminal. He held up a sign and Garrett saw his name printed in large letters. He raised his hand as he walked toward the harried driver.

"I'm Mr. Sloan."

"My apologies for my lateness, sir. Your original driver was involved in an accident, and I'm a last-minute replacement. My name is Semih and I'm from Efendi Travel."

"No worries. I only just arrived. I hope the other driver wasn't hurt?"

Semih took the handle of Garrett's large suitcase and started walking. "No, no. More damage to the vehicle than him."

They exited the arrivals hall. As he stepped outside the glass doors, natural air hit Garrett. After breathing the canned oxygen of the airplane, the freshness was a pleasant change. The temperature was probably hovering around twelve degrees centigrade, which was quite comfortable for March. Looking up into a blue sky was a nice change from the gray visage he was used to back home. Semih led him toward the area where a bunch of taxis waited. They reached a white Mercedes minivan and Semih opened the rear passenger door. Garrett stood by while Semih loaded his luggage then climbed in.

PUBLISHING

Sign up for our newsletter and find out about all our romance book releases, eBook sales and promotions, sneak peeks and FREE romance eBooks!

About the Author

If you look up the word conundrum in the dictionary, there should be Trina's photo next to the description. Her multifaceted personality has left her friends scratching their heads in wonder. A scientist with a passion for history, music and photography she loves to travel and experience new places but is terminally shy around people she doesn't know.

Trina has been devouring romance novels since her tender teenage years. In 2007 she finally took the initiative to write down one of stories that had been rattling around her head for years. Her choices in reading and writing material are as diverse as her iTunes library, which contains music from Mozart to Metallica. Her one concession is all stories must have a happily ever after ending. Did we mention she's incurably romantic?

Trina loves to hear from readers. You can find her contact information, website details and author profile page at https://www.pride-publishing.com